Born in England in 1970, Santa Montefiore grew up in Hampshire. She is married to writer Simon Sebag Montefiore. They live with their two children, Lily and Sasha, in London.

The Kiss

Santa Montefiore

**SIMON &
SCHUSTER**

London · New York · Sydney · Toronto · New Delhi

First published in Great Britain by Simon & Schuster UK Ltd, 2022

1 3 5 7 9 10 8 6 4 2

Simon & Schuster UK Ltd
1st Floor
222 Gray's Inn Road
London WC1X 8HB

Simon & Schuster Australia, Sydney
Simon & Schuster India, New Delhi

www.simonandschuster.co.uk
www.simonandschuster.com.au
www.simonandschuster.co.in

A CIP catalogue record for this book
is available from the British Library

Paperback ISBN: 978-1-3985-0554-4
eBook ISBN: 978-1-3985-0555-1
Audio ISBN: 978-1-3985-1882-7

Typeset in Stone Serif by M Rules
Printed and bound by CPI Group (UK) Ltd, Croydon, CR0 4YY

MIX
Paper from
responsible sources
FSC® C171272

To my daughter, Lilochka, with love.

Chapter 1

The letter

1995, Apple Tree House, Hampshire

Robert Seymour was sitting at the breakfast table in the garden room, reading the newspaper and sipping a cup of coffee, when the letter arrived. Up until that moment it had been a normal Saturday morning at Apple Tree House. Robert had taken the dogs for their walk at eight, leaving his wife Elizabeth asleep in their big, super king-sized bed. He had enjoyed listening to the birdsong and watching the woods emerge from their winter sleep as his two black spaniels charged through the undergrowth, disturbing the odd pheasant or hare.

It was early spring, his favourite time of year, and plucky little shoots were appearing everywhere he looked. Robert returned an hour later to find his eldest son, Jack, already at the breakfast table, tucking into a large plate of eggs and bacon on toast. Jack was twenty-five and home for the weekend from London, where he worked at Sotheby's auction house. Robert's two other sons were still in bed and would likely stay there until midday.

The letter sat on the hall table during breakfast, ignored. Robert drank his coffee, ate two slices of marmalade toast and grunted crossly over an article in the newspaper, but generally he was in a good mood. He was sixty-two, fit and handsome, successful and wealthy. He had a beautiful wife ten years his junior and three healthy sons who still enjoyed the company of their parents. He was blessed. He couldn't deny it. He was very, very lucky.

The letter might have been ignored for the entire morning had it not been for Elizabeth, Robert's wife, who brought it into the garden room with her cup of tea. It was hidden among a few boring brown envelopes and one or two catalogues from Elizabeth's favourite shops. She put her teacup on the table, swept her dressing gown beneath her and slid onto the long seat with a sigh.

'Morning, darling,' Elizabeth said to her son, idly looking through the post. 'Did you sleep well?'

'Like a log,' Jack replied, pouring himself another cup of coffee.

Elizabeth looked out of the window. 'Beautiful day,' she said with a smile, as the garden was indeed bright with sunshine. 'Did the dogs enjoy their walk?' she said to her husband.

Robert barely lifted his eyes off the page. 'They terrorised the wildlife, as usual,' he mumbled.

Elizabeth placed the catalogues beside her plate. She frowned when she saw the letter. It was a plain white envelope, addressed to Robert Seymour in blue, girlish writing she did not recognise. 'This one's for you,' she said, holding it out. Robert took it and glanced at it. Thinking it must be from a godchild, he left it on the table and continued to read the newspaper.

It wasn't until the very end of breakfast, when Elizabeth had gone upstairs to change and Jack and Robert were left alone at the table, planning a game of golf, that Robert opened the envelope with a knife. He pulled the letter out and unfolded it. His eyes read the first line. It took a great deal of self-control not to cry out, gasp or swear. Instead, he folded it calmly and put it back in the envelope, hoping his son did not notice his trembling fingers or the blood draining from his face. 'Let's set off at ten,' he said, getting up. 'There are one or two things I need to do in my study first.'

As Robert walked across the hall to his study

he felt as if he were wading through concrete. He looked steady, calm even, yet his heart thumped against his ribcage like a magpie in a trap, throwing itself against the bars. He closed the study door behind him and sank into a leather chair with a groan. He swept his hand over his forehead – which was now damp with sweat – and sat a moment with the letter in his hand, as still as a statue. This letter would change everything.

Eventually, he slipped it out of the envelope and read it. He had known it would come one day, but had hoped that something might happen to prevent it. Nothing had, for here it was. Her handwriting was real. *She* was real and there was nothing he could do about it. His eyes took in the words and, as he digested them, he knew he only had himself to blame.

Dear Mr Seymour,

My name is Madison. I am your daughter. My mother, Alice Flynn, has given me your name, having promised for as long as I can remember that the identity of my real father would be revealed to me on my eighteenth birthday. I'm sorry if this has come out of the blue, or shocked you, but, as you have financially supported me since I was born, I know that you will have probably been expecting me to contact you around now. I would also love to meet you. My details are at the top of this letter and I very much hope that you will reply.

  Yours sincerely, Madison

Robert stuffed the letter into the envelope and got up from his chair. He felt sick, as if he were in a little boat rising and falling on the waves. He staggered over to his desk where he kept a china dish full of knick-knacks and loose change. He burrowed about for the key to unlock the top right-hand drawer of his desk. He placed the envelope at the very bottom of the drawer, beneath a pile of important papers. This time when he locked it, he hid the key inside the cover of a David Bowie album stacked among his favourite CDs in the bookcase. His wife was not a fan of David Bowie.

Robert Seymour's Saturday had been ruined. What had started as a normal day had turned into the most abnormal day in his entire life. He needed air. He needed to be outside in the garden, among the birdsong and the budding trees and bushes, and he needed to be alone. He did not even take the dogs. He hurried through the house, hoping that Elizabeth wouldn't detain him in the hall, or call him back as he left by the back door. He held his breath, crept as quietly as he could and snuck out, leaving two confused little faces behind the door. They were wondering why he had left them inside when he always took them with him into the garden.

Robert hurried towards the vegetable garden, which was hidden behind an old brick and flint wall. As soon as he was out of sight of the house, and Elizabeth's sharp vision, he took a deep breath. He sank onto a wooden bench and put his head in his hands. *Oh Lord*, he sighed, *what have I got myself into?*

But there was no point beating himself up about a brief one-night stand he'd had eighteen years ago on a business trip in New York. He remembered her now. Alice Flynn, a young journalist staying in the same hotel to interview a well-known film director. What was done was done.

He couldn't go back and *un*do it. He couldn't even hide it. Evidence of his extramarital fling was about to burst onto his peaceful family life like a volcano that has been dormant for eighteen years suddenly exploding into lava and flame. *Oh Lord*, he groaned. *What am I to do?*

He couldn't remember much about Alice Flynn. She'd been young and pretty, of course, but even her prettiness had faded from memory.

He wouldn't have remembered her at all if she hadn't contacted him nine months later with the horrendous news that she had given birth to his child, a little girl. She'd named her Madison after the street near the hotel where she'd been conceived.

Robert had been left no alternative than to pay Alice off. Anything to keep her quiet. Anything to save his marriage and his happy family life – by then he and Elizabeth had been married for nine years and had three enchanting boys. He'd agreed to pay a monthly allowance for the child's upkeep.

He'd said nothing about meeting her once she turned eighteen. But he didn't blame Madison for wanting to know her father. It was just a question of whether he could keep his daughter a secret. Did Elizabeth have to know?

'Dad!' It was Jack, calling him for golf. He looked at his watch. It was past ten. He got up and made towards the door in the wall.

It was going to be fine, he told himself. He'd write back and suggest a meeting in London. They'd have lunch or, even better, tea, and his family wouldn't have to know anything about it.

Chapter 2

Madison

It had been a week since Madison had written the letter. Every morning she waited for the post, hoping that he had written back. She listened out for the telephone too, just in case he chose to call. She had left both her address and telephone number at the top of the page. 'Don't worry, he'll get in touch,' her mother reassured Madison. 'He won't want you turning up on his doorstep.'

Madison had not wanted to alarm him by writing the letter. She knew he was married and had three sons who were all older than her. It was obvious that his wife had no idea of Madison's existence. Madison wasn't about to upset her by turning up and exposing her husband as an adulterer. She just wanted to know where she came from.

Her mother had told her on her eighteenth birthday that she had been conceived during a night of passion in New York. Alice had been a young English freelance journalist writing an article for *Vanity Fair*. By then Robert Seymour was already a successful TV producer. Now, of course, he had his own production company.

Back then her mother had known he was married. She hadn't wanted anything more than a fun night with Robert, she claimed. At the age of twenty-eight, she'd certainly not wanted to get pregnant. Robert was handsome in a very English way: fair-haired with denim-blue eyes, a long, straight nose and a charming smile.

Alice told Madison that he'd had a way with the ladies, a wicked twinkle in his eye, and she had assumed he'd probably cheated on his wife before. They had had a late-night drink in the bar. He had spent the day in meetings and was looking for entertainment. After a few cocktails and a lot of flirting, they had weaved their way up to his room. He had a suite, Alice recalled. She had been impressed. The following morning, they had breakfast together – room service, which was exciting for Alice, who wasn't used to that sort of luxury. Then they had parted as friends.

Nine months later, Madison was born. Alice had tracked Robert down, which hadn't been difficult, as he was a high-profile person. He had been very good about it, although the shock had likely been immense. They had met in London, at a coffee shop in Covent Garden, and made a deal. Robert had been generous, as she knew he would be. He had too much to lose by being stingy.

'You look like your father,' her mother said. 'Blonde, blue-eyed. And you both love films. I'm sure you'll get on like a house on fire.'

Alice understood why Madison wanted to meet her biological father. Although she didn't feel it was necessary. She had married when Madison was three years old and Madison had three siblings. Tom, Alice's husband, had been a wonderful father to her. He had never made her feel less than his own children. To Tom, Madison was his daughter.

The only contribution Robert had made to her life, besides co-creating it, was monthly payments. Tom was the one who had read her bedtime stories, played with her in the garden, built her a Wendy house from scratch. He had kissed her grazed knee when she fell off her bike and wrapped his big arms around her when she needed comfort.

Alice would have preferred Madison not to have written that letter to Robert, but she hadn't tried to stop her. Madison would meet him in London, they would have an awkward tea somewhere grand, and that would be that. Robert would want nothing more to do with her and, as she was now eighteen, the payments had stopped. He had kept his side of the bargain. It was a relationship that wasn't going to go anywhere. How could it?

Madison gazed at herself in the mirror, as she had done over the years, and tried to find traces of her real father. Her mother had never kept him secret. Madison had known Tom wasn't her natural father for as long as she could remember, in the same way that she had known Joe, Becky and Elsie weren't her full siblings. Her mother had never made a big deal out of it, so Madison hadn't either. However, she had searched her features for him, this mystery man who had brought her into the world, every time she looked in the glass.

Madison stared at herself now. She knew she had his blue eyes, because her mother had told her. Alice had brown eyes. Robert was also fair, like Madison. Alice was dark-haired and olive-skinned. In fact, when Madison stared at her reflection she was sure that she saw her father staring back at her, because she barely saw her mother at all.

Another morning went by and no letter arrived

from Robert Seymour. Madison, who was studying for her A Levels, tried to concentrate. However, it was impossible to think of anything else but the letter that never came. Had she written her address clearly on the envelope? Had she made a mistake with the telephone number? Maybe he was on holiday and hadn't even received it.

She closed her file and walked down to the beach. It was a short walk if she cut across a field. Normally she would have taken pleasure from the buttercups and cow parsley but today she felt sad. If she never got to meet her real father, she'd only ever know half of herself.

Madison had lived in Devon all her life. She'd been to London a few times and there had been a few family holidays to Spain, but money was tight with four children in tow. Tom and Alice didn't have the means to splash out on unnecessary luxuries. She knew the money Robert paid for her upkeep was generous, and that Alice had asked for more – and had been given it – when Madison had started secondary school.

Madison suspected her allowance was shared with her other siblings and probably paid for the odd designer coat or handbag her mother returned with after a shopping trip to London. But Madison didn't mind. She was creative and dreamy and more interested in painting and reading than in fashion.

A week later, when she had almost given up on ever hearing from Robert Seymour, a letter arrived in the post. It was written on blue paper, with his address printed at the top of the page. It was signed simply: Robert. Madison managed to slip out of the house and down to the beach without anyone noticing. She wanted to read it alone. Tucked out of the wind behind rocks, she unfolded it.

Dear Madison,

Thank you for your letter. I am, indeed, your father. As I'm sure your mother told you, I am married with three sons and have no wish to upset their lives by telling them about you. Therefore, let us tread with care and tact. I would very much like to meet you.

Would it be possible for you to come to London? I'll send you the train ticket and invite you for lunch at Le Caprice in St James's. Let me know a good day that works for you. Until then, I send you my best wishes.

Yours, Robert

Madison could barely believe it. She read the letter over and over again, analysing each sentence, searching for meaning between the lines. She was aware that she would only get one lunch with him. By mentioning his wife and children, Robert had made it quite clear that he had no desire for a relationship with her. But it didn't matter. All she wanted was to meet him, then she'd feel complete.

She pressed the letter to her heart and gazed out over the sparkling water. Yes, she'd be complete once she knew her father. All her life she had felt there was something missing. Like there was an empty space somewhere inside her chest that nothing could fill. Every time she was hurt, or angry, or let down, she would hug her pillow and tell herself that if she had a real father, like Joe, Becky and Elsie, she would be perfectly content. She loved Tom, but she didn't belong to him. How she yearned to belong to Robert.

In the days that led up to her trip to London, Madison thought of nothing but Robert Seymour. She invested all her dreams in him. They would have so much in common, she knew. They would laugh at the same things, love the same things, and see themselves reflected in the other.

She didn't consider what would happen if the lunch was a massive disappointment – if they had nothing in common but their blue eyes. She couldn't bear to prepare herself for that.

Chapter 3

The meeting

Robert awoke in his London flat with a heavy sense of dread. Today was the day he was due to meet his daughter. He lay in bed, staring at the grey light that trickled through the gaps in the blind, and wished it were tonight already. He was not looking forward to meeting her. He did not want to think about that night in New York. It only filled him with shame. How could he have been so foolish? What had he been thinking?

When Alice had telephoned his office and told him he had a daughter, he had nearly had a heart attack. The faces of his wife and sons had floated before him like bubbles about to burst and disappear for ever. Panicked by the thought of losing them, he had paid Alice. That was what she had wanted. She hadn't demanded that he play a role in the child's life, or publicly recognise her, which was a great relief. So he had swiftly arranged a monthly payment and hoped the whole thing would go away. It had for eighteen years, but now the problem was back.

He groaned and climbed out of bed. He would have a quick lunch with Madison, say all the right things and then head back to Elizabeth and the boys in Hampshire. No one would be any the wiser. He could brush his dirty little secret under the carpet again.

Robert's office was in a pretty white townhouse in St James's, Mayfair. It was a small but very successful company, making some of the most popular English sitcoms. Robert was able to lose himself in work and not think about the dreaded lunch, until the time arrived and he left the building, dragging his feet like a schoolboy heading for the exam hall.

It was an overcast day. Thick clouds hung low over the city, threatening rain. He arrived at Le Caprice and was greeted by the Bolivian manager, Jesus, who knew him well, as Robert often ate there. 'Good afternoon, Mr Seymour,' said Jesus, smiling warmly. 'Your guest is yet to arrive.'

'Good,' Robert replied. He would order a stiff drink and compose himself. 'Just a quick lunch with a goddaughter,' he added, then wished he hadn't, because it sounded guilty. When had he ever explained a guest to Jesus?

He was given the corner table by the window,

as usual. A table for two, looking into the room. The restaurant was busy. He ordered a Martini, straight up. It didn't bother him that he knew one or two of the other diners. Better to hide in plain sight, he always thought. Much guiltier to be discovered in a discreet little restaurant somewhere off the beaten track.

His Martini arrived and he gulped it down. God, he had a daughter. It was surreal. It also made him feel a little queasy. Still, just because she was his blood didn't mean they were going to have anything in common. The lunch was going to be agonising, he knew it. At least he would order something good to eat. He trailed his eyes over the menu, even though he knew it by heart.

As he was reading the specials, he was interrupted by Jesus. 'Your guest has arrived, Mr Seymour.'

Robert looked up. Standing before him, smiling nervously, was Madison.

They stared at each other. Robert stood up and shook her hand. He was pleasantly surprised. Madison was very pretty with long tousled blonde hair, intelligent blue eyes and a gentle, sensitive mouth. His first impression was of innocence and purity. The heaviness that he had been carrying in his belly all morning dissolved.

'I'm so sorry I'm late,' she said. Her voice was soft and husky, like brown sugar. 'The train was late.'

'Trains are always late,' said Robert, watching her take a seat in the chair that Jesus pulled out for her. 'Unless, of course, you're in Switzerland, when they are always on time. To the second.'

She laughed and put her handbag on the floor. 'Thank you for agreeing to meet me.'

Her clear gaze disarmed him. 'It's a pleasure,' he replied. 'It's right that we meet, now you're eighteen. Thank *you* for coming all the way up from Devon.' He had expected to resent her, to rush through lunch and leave as soon as was politely possible. To his surprise, he found that he was already enjoying her company. 'Would you like a glass of wine?' he asked.

'Thank you, I'd love one,' she replied, trying to act as if lunch at Le Caprice and a glass of wine were perfectly normal. Under the table, out of sight, her legs trembled.

Her mother had been right. She and Robert did, indeed, have the same blue eyes. She looked at him, searching for herself, but hoping not to reveal too much curiosity. He had a nice face, handsome but above all kind. It was the face of someone who was honest and decent, not the face of someone capable of betraying his

18

wife and sleeping with a stranger in a hotel in New York.

Madison, being young and inexperienced, did not detect, as her mother had eighteen years before, the cheeky twinkle in his eye. To Madison he was, so far, everything she'd hoped he would be.

They studied the menu. Robert was the perfect gentleman, giving Jesus her choices and ordering a bottle of sparkling water. 'I always think sparkling is more festive. Still water we can get from the tap,' he told her.

Then he asked her about herself. He hadn't expected to be interested, but he discovered, to his joy, that he was very interested indeed. 'I love books,' Madison said. Robert also loved books. In fact, some of his best television series had been adapted from books.

'Who are your favourite authors?' he asked.

'Oh, there are so many. Let me see.' She bit her lip and fiddled with her knife before checking herself and withdrawing her hand. 'I've read all Daphne du Maurier's and Jane Austen. I mean, they're classics, aren't they? I've been reading *The Remains of the Day* by Kazuo Ishiguro. It's beautiful. I've almost finished, but I wanted to save some for the train ride home.'

*

The food came and went. They ordered dessert. Madison felt light-headed after one glass of wine. Robert was sober after a Martini and the rest of the bottle of Sancerre. They were so deep in conversation that they didn't notice the dining room grow quieter as the other diners finished their lunch and left. Madison's legs stopped trembling and she put her elbow on the table and rested her chin on her hand as they moved on to talk about art and film and theatre.

For an eighteen-year-old, Madison knew a lot about the arts, and was clearly passionate about them. Robert was fascinated. Of his sons, only Jack was interested in those things and as a result worked at Sotheby's auction house. His other two sons were far keener on sport.

Robert was cheered to find that his daughter loved all the things he did. He was inspired, suddenly, by this child who loved theatre but rarely had the opportunity to go. Who loved literature, but had to wait for books to come out in the cheaper paperback.

He decided he didn't want their relationship to end on the pavement outside the restaurant. He wanted it to continue. He wanted to nurture her. To take her to the London theatres, to the ballet, the opera and the movies. To send her books and enjoy long lunches discussing them. Now he'd found her, he didn't want to let her go.

'Would you like to walk around the park?' he suggested, noticing the empty dining room. The waiters were hovering to clear their table and knock off for the afternoon.

Madison looked at her watch. 'I suppose I could get a later train,' she said. Then she grinned and Robert was sure he could see traces of his mother in her smile. 'Are you sure you haven't had enough of me by now?'

'Absolutely not,' he replied, grinning back. 'I'm only just getting started.'

Chapter 4

The secret

That evening, after seeing Madison on to the train at Paddington, Robert returned to his flat with a bounce in his step. What a surprising day it had turned out to be. Having not wanted to meet her, in the end he hadn't wanted to let her go. He could not have predicted that. In fact, he found he rather liked the idea of having a daughter.

Madison. He even liked the name. It was unique, just like her. How he longed to share her with Elizabeth and the boys. Indeed, the fear that had haunted him for the last eighteen years now receded. He was sure they would love Madison if they got to know her.

But could Elizabeth ever forgive him for cheating on her? Robert wasn't ready to test her powers of forgiveness. The gamble was too great – and he had too much to lose.

The following day Robert went into work. After

a morning meeting with marketing people he set about choosing some books he thought Madison might like. He took his time, considering each one carefully. Then he gave them to his secretary to send to Devon.

He sat at his desk and tapped the tip of his pen against his chin. He wanted to do more. Besides the monthly allowance, which had stopped on her eighteenth birthday, he had done nothing. No birthday presents, Christmas presents or any kind of message at all. He felt bad about that now.

Well, he decided, taking his cheque book out of his drawer, he would start to put that right. He didn't want to embarrass her by giving her too much, but he was aware he had eighteen birthdays and Christmases to make up for. He should also invite her to the theatre or to the Royal Opera House – something special.

Writing a cheque seemed lazy and a little thoughtless. Yet he couldn't invite her anywhere for fear of being spotted by someone he knew – and besides, she lived in Devon. Right now, money was the only thing he could give her.

Madison had returned home on a high. Not only had she met her father, but they had got on so well that he had invited her to walk round the park so they could talk some more. She was bursting to share her excitement, but she didn't want to upset Tom by raving about her *real* father. She knew Tom loved her like a daughter. She was also wary about sharing her feelings with her siblings. After all, their father had raised her as his own while Robert had done nothing but send money every month.

Then there was Alice. Her mother had not been wildly keen on her contacting Robert in the first place. She might feel uneasy about Madison having a relationship with this man whom Alice had only met once and didn't know. It was better, she decided, that she keep the events of the day to herself.

When Madison had arrived home, her mother had asked her how it had gone and Madison had replied simply. It had been very nice to meet him, she'd told her. They'd enjoyed a lovely lunch at Le Caprice and got on very well. 'Are you going to see him again?' her mother had asked.

'I doubt it,' Madison had answered, although she knew that was a lie. Robert had told her that he had every intention of making up for the years he had missed, and she believed him.

Now she was sitting on the beach with another letter in her hand. However, it wasn't the letter that surprised her this time, but the cheque that had slipped out of it. It was a great deal of money. More money than she had ever had, including the thousand pounds she had earned the summer before, working as a nanny for a local family. This was the sort of money one put away in the bank and saved for something special, like travelling or university expenses.

She pressed the cheque to her chest and sighed with happiness. Robert might not have been in her life for eighteen years, but it looked like he was going to be very much present for the rest.

Madison decided she wasn't going to tell Tom or her mother about the money. Even though Robert was her father, they might think it strange that a man she had only just met was writing her big cheques. Also, Tom worked for a tent business and didn't earn the sort of money Robert did, which might make him feel inadequate. He'd always been generous to Madison. How would it make him feel to know that Robert had given her thousands of pounds with one swipe of his pen?

As for Alice, her mother might feel that Madison didn't deserve it and make her share it with the family. When it came to money, everything was always shared equally among the children. There was no doubt in Madison's mind that this was the kind of money that could upset the apple cart. They were a close family, and

Madison did not want to create discord where there was none.

And so it was, with tact and discretion, that Robert Seymour and Madison Honeywell set about building a father–daughter relationship. Robert, keen to make up for all the years he had neglected her, bought a small flat in Queensgate where she could stay when she was in London. He took her out to lunch and even managed to invite her to the ballet and the theatre without bumping into anyone who might question what he was doing with a pretty young girl under half his age.

Madison told her family she was staying with a friend and, because she was over eighteen, no one questioned her. She worked hard for her A Levels and got the grades to start university in Bristol that September, studying English Literature.

Robert insisted on helping her with her university expenses. She tried to refuse, telling him that he had already been generous enough. But he put a gentle hand on hers and said, 'I'm your father, Madison. Supporting you financially is something a father should do. But I can tell you, honestly, I'm not doing it out of duty, but because I want to.' And she couldn't argue with that.

Robert and Elizabeth spent the summer at their vineyard in Tuscany, as they did every year, and their three boys came and went and invited friends and girlfriends as they always did. The days were long and lazy, the sun hot, beating down upon the rows of vines, the olive groves, the tall pines and gardens overflowing with blossom. Robert wished he could invite Madison to stay. He knew she'd love it there at Villa Aurora. But one look at his wife and sons convinced him, every time he longed for it, that it simply wasn't worth the risk.

Three years passed in the same manner, and Robert grew deeply fond of Madison. She graduated from university with a first-class degree, and Robert gave her a job in his company. It was a lowly job, but she'd work her way up and, who knows, one day she might even take over from him.

Perhaps it was that thought, or because he was tired of keeping her secret, that gave him the outrageous idea to tell Elizabeth the truth. Whichever it was, on a rainy morning in March, when he and Elizabeth were alone at Apple Tree House, Robert put down the newspaper and turned to his wife. He looked at her across the breakfast table and said, 'My darling, I have something I need to tell you.'

Chapter 5

The gamble

Elizabeth stared at her husband. Robert stared back, astonished that the words he had hidden for twenty-one years had at last been spoken. Part of him felt a massive sense of relief, the other half anxiety, which grew more intense as he watched his wife's face drain of blood. She slowly put down her teacup. With forced calmness, she asked him to repeat what he had just told her, and to tell her the whole story.

When he had finished, she got up from the table. 'I need time to digest this,' was all she said before disappearing upstairs. Robert knew not to follow her, not to beg her forgiveness or attempt to justify his actions. In fact, he knew not to do anything at all. Elizabeth needed time, and she needed to be alone.

He climbed into his car and drove up to London.

*

Elizabeth watched him go from her bedroom window. Then she sank onto the bed and stared into space. She was in shock. Not only had her husband confessed to having committed adultery, he had told her that his betrayal had resulted in a daughter, who was now twenty-two years old. How was she meant to feel? Let down? Humiliated? She didn't know. She felt nothing, just numbness, as if her heart had suddenly got cold and lost all feeling.

She climbed back into bed. She put the blanket over her head and closed her eyes. Her husband and best friend, the man she thought she knew better than anyone else in the world, had turned into a stranger over breakfast. And if *he* had been someone else all along, then so had she. They had *both* been living a lie.

The logic was very simple: she clearly wasn't enough for him. He had admitted to betraying her once, and it was likely that there were many other betrayals he was not admitting to. He had probably slept with lots of women during their marriage. Which meant that she wasn't beautiful, attractive or sexy, as she had believed, but lacking.

Yes, she was lacking, she decided, because Robert had had to search for the qualities that she was missing in other women. As the solid ground of her marriage turned to mush, she sobbed into her pillow, feeling every bit of her fifty-five years: dowdy, middle-aged and past it.

Eventually, she got dressed and went for a walk with the dogs. It was drizzling, which Elizabeth found comforting. It would have been an insult had the sun shone in the face of her misery. Her wellington boots stomped through the long grass as the spaniels ran into the undergrowth where bright green shoots were emerging from the sodden ground.

She thrust her hands into her coat pockets and took a deep breath. The past was done, and there was nothing she could do to change it. The question was, what was she going to do about it *now*?

Elizabeth knew that her actions had the power to break up the family or keep it together. It would be all too easy to ask for a divorce, to throw away thirty years of marriage and play the part of the wronged wife. But Elizabeth had never been a coward, and the label 'victim' was not one she wanted to carry. What good would a divorce do anyway? The boys would be devastated, and where would it leave her? She loved Robert. She didn't much like the thought of spending the rest of her life without him.

Elizabeth got to the top of the hill and stood

staring out over the fields that rose and fell in gentle curves as far as the eye could see. She put a hand on her heart, feeling a little better as she always did from seeing the beauty of the natural world. She felt the power within her to either create or destroy, and as a shaft of sunlight broke through the cloud, Elizabeth knew which she would choose.

There was only one thing to do. As she set off back down the hill, she was suddenly filled with confidence, because the choice was *hers* and she felt a sense of being in control again. Elizabeth was taking back the power and deciding what would happen.

She'd leave Robert stewing for a few days. She wasn't about to let him off the hook. He had done wrong and he needed to earn Elizabeth's forgiveness. However, the one person who was innocent in all of this, and who deserved to be treated fairly and with kindness, was Madison.

Robert was desperate. Alone in London, he sat in his study but was unable to put his mind to anything constructive. All he could think about was his wife and the fact that he had hurt her. He hated himself for having caused her suffering. He worried that he'd done the wrong thing in coming clean.

Had he been selfish in telling her? Perhaps he should have thought more about Elizabeth's feelings and how the news would affect *her*, and less about Madison and his desire to bring their relationship into the open.

Suddenly, he was gripped by fear. He didn't want to lose Elizabeth. He couldn't imagine life without her. The more he thought about her, the more he realised how important she was not only to him, as his wife and companion, but to the family. If she decided to leave him, he'd lose his sons as well, as they'd never forgive him. The four of them would cut him out of their lives for ever.

Robert didn't hear from Elizabeth for three long days. Every time he went to call her he changed his mind and hung up. He knew his wife. Elizabeth needed time to think. If she wanted to speak to him, she would pick up the phone herself. She obviously didn't. She was angry and hurt, and Robert didn't blame her. He only hoped she would come through it and decide, in the end, that their marriage was worth fighting for.

On the fourth day, the telephone rang. Robert picked it up.

'Hello, Robert,' Elizabeth said. Her tone was dull and cold.

'Hi,' he replied.

'Can you come down? There's something I need to tell you.'

Robert felt sick as she repeated the same words he had said to her at the breakfast table. If she wanted to tell him that it was over, he would have to accept it. After all, Robert only had himself to blame. How could she trust him now, after he had kept such a massive secret from her for so long?

Robert drove straight to Hampshire. When he arrived, Elizabeth was waiting for him in the sitting room. Dressed in a pair of jeans and a grey V-neck sweater, her long brown hair loose, she looked younger than her fifty-five years. She looked like the girl she had been when he met her. His heart flooded with regret and remorse. 'Oh, Elizabeth.' He reached out his hand.

'Sit down, Robert,' she said.

He did as he was told. 'I've had a lot of time to think. You've put me through absolute hell, I won't lie about it. To discover not only that my husband had an affair ...'

'A one-night stand,' he corrected firmly. 'It was only once, Elizabeth.'

'It amounts to the same thing, Robert. One night or many nights, you broke your marriage vows and I'm devastated. But you and this woman brought a child into the world, and it's this child I would like to focus on now. You and I need time to work through this and I think we can. But Madison deserves to have a father who is active in her life. Therefore, I have a proposal to make.'

Robert felt he had just been saved from the hangman's noose.

'I want you to invite her to Italy this summer so we can all meet her and get to know her. If she's going to be a part of your life, I want her to be a part of ours too.'

'Elizabeth ...' Robert wanted to embrace her and thank her for her incredible generosity of spirit. He'd always known she was a fine woman, but only now did he realise just how fine she was.

'I have one condition,' Elizabeth added.

'Yes?'

'That I never have to meet her mother.'

Chapter 6

Villa Aurora

Robert's sons, Jack, Arthur and Hal, arrived at Villa Aurora that summer with mixed feelings. It was one thing to discover that their father had been unfaithful, but quite another to learn that that moment of weakness had brought about a child. It was hard to get their heads around the fact that they had a half-sister – that they'd almost *always* had a half-sister, only never known her – and now she was coming to Italy to meet them.

Jack, the eldest, was particularly resentful of his father. Like his brothers, he was protective of his mother and appalled by his father's betrayal.

His beautiful, model girlfriend of four years, Blythe Moreton, boosted his resentment and made the issue so much worse. She didn't understand why Madison had to come and stay.

'What has she got to do with you, besides sharing a bit of blood?' she complained. 'If I were you, Jack, I'd tell your father that she is *his* business and nothing to do with you. It's *his* affair, *his* child and *his* mess. Why make her your business as well? And just because she's related to you doesn't mean you'll like her. She might be awful and we'll have to put up with her for a whole week!'

Jack tended to agree. He had no desire to meet Madison. He told his parents that he and Blythe were not going to come out to Italy this summer.

Elizabeth, who knew very well who was behind this small act of rebellion, told him sweetly but firmly that his presence was very much expected. Blythe was welcome to stay in the UK if she so wished.

Blythe, anxious not to miss out on glorious Tuscan weather, delicious food and luxury, because Villa Aurora was exceptionally grand, swallowed her objections. She declared that it wouldn't be fair to leave Jack to face his new half-sister alone, and promptly booked her plane ticket to Pisa.

Arthur and Hal, who didn't have girlfriends to poison their minds against their new half-sibling, were intrigued to meet Madison. They rather took their mother's view that what was done was done, and the only thing to do was face up to it, accept it and carry on. Robert was grateful for their understanding. It was a miracle that they were still speaking to him at all. He put it down to Elizabeth's noble example. If she could be so forgiving and generous-spirited, then so could they.

Madison was understandably nervous. She was going to meet Robert's wife and sons, which was terrifying. When she had taken the train to London three years earlier to meet him at Le Caprice, she hadn't thought further than her father. She hadn't considered siblings.

Then, when he had told her that he had three boys, she had never thought she would meet them. They belonged to a different category, separate from Robert, and not important to her quest to find out where she came from. As far as she was concerned, they had nothing to do with her. Besides, she already had a half-brother and two half-sisters from her mother's marriage with Tom.

It was only now, when Robert decided he needed to tell his wife the truth, that he suggested Madison fly out to Italy and meet them all properly. 'I've confessed to Elizabeth and she wants to meet you,' he had told her over lunch.

He had seemed very pleased with his wife's

willingness to accept her. Madison presumed he had probably feared she'd kick him out in disgust. 'She's a very good person,' he had added, looking humbled. 'It was *she* who suggested you meet the boys. I would never have dared mention it, but Elizabeth brought it up on her own. She's a far better person than me.'

Now Madison sat in the taxi, being driven out of Pisa by an Italian who spoke no English, in a car that smelt of garlic and body odour. It was hot. The fierce midday sun streamed through the open window, turning the pale skin on her forearm pink. The driver, a short man with curly black hair and a tattoo of a red heart with the word *Mamma* written across it on his hand, sang along to the radio.

Madison's stomach churned. She had no idea what to expect. Elizabeth had been generous to invite her, of course, but it didn't mean she was going to embrace her into the bosom of the family. They must all hate her, she thought. She was proof of Robert's betrayal. How could they possibly like her?

Villa Aurora was an hour and a half's drive from Pisa airport. The taxi turned off the main highway and motored up quiet country roads that wound past fields of vines and hillsides of olive groves. Madison had never been to Italy before and she gazed in wonder at the beauty of the landscape, the fields full of sunflowers and poppies. The ancient churches that dominated the villages. It was the kind of beauty that broke the heart. But Madison was too nervous to allow it to move hers. Had she been in a less anxious frame of mind, Tuscany would already have held her captive.

At last the driver turned into the entrance of the villa. The iron gates were wide open, revealing a dirt track that led up a hill through an avenue of inky green cypress trees. Glimpsing through the trees, Madison could see the gardens. The sight of pink bougainvillea and lavender lifted her spirits.

They pulled up outside the big door. Madison was sweating with heat and nerves and wished she could take a shower before meeting the family. She paid the driver, who lifted her suitcase out of the boot and carried it up the steps to the door. Then he was off down the hill, leaving a trail of dust behind him.

Madison gazed about her, wishing she hadn't come. The villa was beautiful but frightening. Decorated with giant terracotta pots of lemon trees and manicured hedges, it was the kind of place you paid to visit, like a stately home or a hotel, not the kind of place you lived in. It had been one thing getting to know Robert, but she wasn't sure she wanted to be part of his family. If they were anything like this villa, she wouldn't fit in at all.

She went to the door and searched for a bell. There didn't seem to be one. An enormous round knocker looked more decorative than practical, but as it was the only option, she lifted it and let it bang loudly against the iron. When no one came, she left her bag on the step and wandered round to see if anyone was in the garden.

The air was thick with the scent of jasmine and honeysuckle, and the sound of birdsong rang out of the pine trees. It was peaceful and pretty and delightfully exotic to Madison, who had left London on a damp and drizzly morning. However, her stomach cramped with nerves and she felt like an intruder.

At last she spotted a woman in a sunhat and white sundress gardening in a border. Madison assumed she must be Elizabeth and walked quickly across the lawn. The woman sensed her approach and stood up. When she saw Madison, she smiled, and Madison relaxed a little in the warmth of it.

'You must be Madison,' the other woman said, pushing through the plants. She took off her gardening glove and put out her hand.

Madison shook it. 'Yes, I am. It's very nice to meet you.'

Elizabeth pushed her sunglasses onto her head, revealing deep-set hazel eyes that shone with goodness. Madison understood at once why this woman had been so generous towards her wayward husband. She seemed kind and wise.

'I'm Elizabeth. I'm sorry no one was in the house to meet you,' she said. 'I didn't hear the taxi. Come with me and let's get you a cold drink and introduce you to the rest of the family. They're down at the pool. It's lovely to meet you. Robert has told me so much about you.'

Madison followed Elizabeth across the lawn to the back of the villa. 'The garden is beautiful,' she said, stepping into the shade of a large fig tree.

Elizabeth wiped her brow and sighed. 'It takes a lot of work, but I do have help. Are you a keen gardener?'

'I love gardens, but don't have one of my own. I have a balcony full of potted plants. But I visit gardens that are open to the public whenever I can.'

'Well, you'll like it here then. Tuscany is one enormous garden.'

It was cool inside, out of the sun, and decorated in whites and natural colours, which gave the place a feeling of calm. Elizabeth dropped her gloves and secateurs into a basket by the door and went on through the villa to the kitchen. There she poured Madison a glass of lemonade from the fridge.

She then collected her bag from the front door and showed her to her room. It was on the first floor with two large windows looking out over the garden and framed by long white linen curtains. 'This is lovely,' Madison exclaimed, gazing down on to the terrace where a table and chairs were arranged in the shade of a vine.

'I'm glad you like it,' said Elizabeth. 'Would you like to freshen up? Or shall we go straight to the pool?'

'Let's go to the pool,' said Madison. She didn't think there was any point in delaying the agony. Meeting Robert's sons was likely to be agonising.

'Bring your bathing suit. It's a bit of a walk and you don't want to have to come all the way back for it.' Madison rootled inside her bag for her swimsuit. She looked forward to cooling off in the water. Then she drained her glass of lemonade and followed Elizabeth back down the stairs.

Chapter 7

Three new brothers

The walk to the pool was down a path that cut through the long grasses. Ahead, the Tuscan hills rolled in gentle curves and folds as far as the eye could see. Madison inhaled the sensual smells of pine and wild rosemary that grew in enormous heaps, their pretty violet flowers attracting bees. She marvelled at the beauty of this magical place. Even if the boys took a dislike to her, she was happy she had come. It was worth it just to walk down this path through paradise.

Soon, the pool came into view. It was built onto a terrace cut into the hillside. Beside the pool were sun loungers with blue and white stripy cushions and towels. Upon them, shiny bronzed bodies soaked up the sun. It was a lazy scene. Quiet and peaceful in the afternoon heat, and Madison felt awkward interrupting it.

'Wakey-wakey, everyone,' Elizabeth called.

'Madison has arrived.' Madison cringed as the bodies slowly stirred.

Robert, who had been asleep in the shade with his panama hat pulled low over his face, got up with a start. 'Madison!' he exclaimed. 'How lovely that you're here.'

Madison went to greet him, allowing him to pull her into his arms and plant two sweaty kisses on her cheeks. Robert was wearing a long white linen shirt over shorts and smelt strongly of lemon cologne.

Three boys made their way slowly across the stone like wary lions. They were wearing Bermuda shorts and sunglasses and were oily and tanned, if a little red on the shoulders. The tallest put out his hand. 'Hi, I'm Jack,' he said. Madison shook it. She noticed he didn't take off his sunglasses. She wondered whether he was examining her behind them, searching for common features that proved they shared the same blood. He swept a hand through tousled brown hair, pushing it off his forehead.

'It's lovely to meet you.' She smiled, covering up her discomfort with faked confidence. As she did so, she noticed his warm expression. 'I'm sorry I disturbed your siestas,' she added to all of them. 'You looked so contented out there.'

Arthur was shorter than Jack, with a round face

and curly brown hair. He grinned in a friendly way and shook her hand warmly. 'Welcome to the family,' he said. 'Nothing like being thrown in at the deep end, is there?'

Madison laughed. His joke defused the tension.

Hal was the most handsome, with his father's big white teeth and his mother's deep-set hazel eyes. He looked her over and didn't try to hide his appreciation. 'Good to meet you, at last,' he said. 'After putting up with the company of two brothers, I welcome the arrival of a sister.'

'Thank you,' she said. 'I grew up with one brother. I never expected I'd have three more. It's really nice to meet you all.'

'Will you go and ask Blythe to come and say hello,' said Elizabeth to Jack. Her tight mouth showed her disapproval. Madison watched Jack wander back out to the lounger where a woman moved lazily. Jack bent down and said something to her. From her body language, Madison could tell she was not happy to be disturbed. Jack took her hand and pulled her off the lounger.

As Blythe walked over, Madison couldn't help but notice her perfect figure in the smallest red bikini she had ever seen. The girl tossed her long, sun-kissed hair but did not take off her shades. As she greeted Madison with an air of boredom, Madison saw her own red face reflected back at her in Blythe's sunglasses. It wasn't a pleasing sight. She wished she had done as Elizabeth had suggested and freshened up before coming down. She wiped the sweat off her nose.

'Put on your swimmers and jump in the pool,' said Robert.

Blythe's pouting lips curled into a smile. 'Yes, come and join us. It's gorgeous in the sun.'

'I think I'll stay in the shade, thank you,' Madison replied. Not only did her skin burn easily, but she was never going to allow her imperfect body to be compared to Blythe in a bathing suit.

Blythe took Jack's hand and tried to escape back to the lounger. Jack caught his mother's eye and pulled it away. 'I could do with a bit of shade too,' he said, although he didn't look very happy about it.

'Me too,' agreed Hal. 'It's been a long day at the office.'

Madison smiled. Hal had a playful twinkle in his eye that appealed to her.

'Lovely,' said Robert, making his way towards the bar. 'What does everyone want to drink?' He looked at his watch. 'It's five o'clock. Not too early for a drink, is it, Elizabeth?'

'On the contrary,' Elizabeth replied for only him to hear. 'I think we all need one.'

Blythe sighed grumpily and went back out to her lounger. Arthur followed Hal to the chairs.

'So, Madison,' said Jack, flopping onto a white sofa and putting his hands behind his head. 'You're our sister. Weird, isn't it? Was it as much of a shock for you as it was for us to learn that Dad was your father?'

'Darling,' interrupted Elizabeth sharply. 'Madison's just arrived. I'm not sure that's the right question to fire at her.'

'Before she's had a drink,' said Hal with a grin. 'Make it strong, Dad. I think she's going to need it.'

'I'm okay,' said Madison, not really feeling okay. It was daunting being faced with three curious young men, openly eyeing her up and down. 'It's natural that you should want to know my side of the story. It's an unusual situation, isn't it?'

'To put it mildly,' said Jack, eyeing his father coldly.

'But we're so happy you're here,' said Elizabeth with some force, and really, if anyone had the right to feel offended, it was Elizabeth.

Madison gratefully took the glass of rosé that Robert offered her. Hal and Arthur were both friendly. Hal, especially, had decided to make light of the situation and cracked jokes at every opportunity. But Madison could tell that Jack was bristling with resentment towards his father. She sensed the sharp edge to his words that were laced with a dry and sarcastic humour.

She didn't imagine he resented *her* personally. How could he? He didn't know her. But he resented his father for having an affair, and for putting him in this position of having to meet the result of that affair. Madison suspected that he hadn't wanted to meet her and that his mother had had to twist his arm. However, she wasn't going to allow his anger towards Robert to sour her time at the villa. It was a beautiful place, and she felt lucky to be here.

The shadows lengthened as the sun sank towards the hills, turning them a rich yellow-orange. The small group chatted in the shade while Blythe dozed in the sun. Elizabeth was clearly cross with her son's girlfriend for not making her guest feel welcome. Every now and then she shot disapproving looks across the pool.

Madison suspected that Blythe might be being tactful, leaving her to get to know her brothers, but then it was in Madison's nature to find the good in everybody. Robert kept refilling their glasses and very soon the atmosphere softened, as did Jack's scornful tone.

'So, which of the Seymour genes have you inherited?' he asked her.

Madison smiled at her father. 'Well, I'm not a gifted tennis player,' she replied.

'We got those,' interrupted Hal. 'There weren't any left for you, I'm afraid.' He shrugged as if to say sorry.

Madison laughed. 'I didn't need them. I wouldn't have had a court to play on anyway. But I love books, theatre, movies and art, like Robert. And painting. That's my real love. If I could wave a magic wand, I'd have a studio somewhere quiet and leafy and paint all day.'

'I didn't know Dad liked painting,' said Arthur, arching an eyebrow in surprise.

'Actually, I was very good at painting as a boy,' said Robert, lifting his chin. 'I might take it up again. Madison's inspired me.'

'I've brought my box of watercolours, if you want to give it a go. There's loads to paint here,' said Madison, letting her gaze wander over the distant rows of vines that covered the opposite hillside.

'Wonderful,' Robert enthused. 'We can set up somewhere quiet and paint the Tuscan hills.'

'That's a lovely idea, darling,' said Elizabeth.

'You could say, then, that you've inherited Dad's creative and intellectual genes,' said Jack.

'Steady on, Jack,' said Arthur. 'You can't say that the three of us don't like art and literature as well. For a start, you work for Sotheby's.'

'What was the last book *you* read?' Jack asked.

'Neil Gaiman, *American Gods*,' Arthur replied, smiling.

Jack turned to Madison and grinned. 'Okay, so you aren't the only one with intellectual genes, you just have a bigger dose.'

'Dad's a producer. Creativity is in all of our genes,' argued Hal. 'And anyway, I'm good at maths. I can't say numbers are Mum or Dad's strong points.' He turned to Madison. 'Are you good at numbers too?'

'Sadly not. I still count on my fingers.'

Elizabeth laughed. 'So do I,' she admitted. 'I've always been terrible at counting. But give me anything to write and I'll have it done in a jiffy.'

Madison liked Elizabeth. She was clearly doing all she could to encourage them to bond, which couldn't have been easy. 'It's not all about genes,' Madison argued. 'Often children are gifted at things their parents can't do, like Hal and maths. People come into the world with their own characters, talents and interests. I don't think we should look to our parents to find out who we are and what we're good at. I think we should just be ourselves.'

'Well said, Madison,' Robert agreed. 'Who knows, if I'd brought you up, perhaps you'd have been a good tennis player, simply for having the opportunity to learn.'

'I'll give you a lesson,' said Jack, draining his glass. 'It'll be interesting to see if you've inherited any coordination at all, or whether . . .'

'I'm afraid, Jack, whether due to nature or nurture, you'll find I'm no tennis player. But I'm happy to be a ball girl instead,' said Madison.

Before Jack could reply, his father cut in, 'And we can all do with one of those.'

Chapter 8

An unexpected suggestion

Madison retreated to her bedroom to unpack and shower. She was relieved. The hardest part was over. She had met the three boys and they had been friendly. Even Jack had warmed up. Only Blythe, Jack's girlfriend, had ignored her.

Blythe had got up from her lounger when they'd left for the house and lagged a short distance behind, holding Jack's hand and keeping him back. Madison had met possessive women like Blythe before. Even though Madison was Jack's sister, it seemed that Blythe felt threatened by her. It was laughable really, Madison thought, as she applied make-up in front of the mirror. Blythe looked like a supermodel. Madison was no threat to her.

Dinner was on the terrace beneath Madison's window. As she sprayed perfume on her wrists, she overheard the boys chatting below.

'She's good-looking,' said Hal. 'If she wasn't my sister, I'd definitely make a play for her.'

'Well, she *is* your sister, so you'd better not,' said Arthur, giving a throaty laugh.

'She's all right,' said Jack. Madison smiled to herself. Well, she was hardly going to score points on the beauty front when compared with Blythe.

'Strange to have a sister, isn't it?' said Arthur. 'I mean, she doesn't feel like my sister.'

'Well of course she doesn't, stupid. You've only just met her,' said Hal. 'She'll probably never feel like our sister. Do you think she's got a boyfriend?'

'Wouldn't know,' said Jack.

'She looks like the sort of girl who would have a boyfriend,' said Arthur.

'What's that supposed to mean?' Jack asked.

'Pretty, but not too pretty. The really beautiful ones frighten men, but the pretty ones are approachable. Those are the ones who are always in relationships,' Arthur replied.

'I didn't find Blythe intimidating,' said Jack.

'Everyone else does,' said Arthur.

Madison drew away from the window. She knew it wasn't wise to eavesdrop. A moment later, Elizabeth's voice joined her sons' voices and they changed the subject. Madison headed downstairs. She bumped into Blythe in the hall.

'Hello,' said Madison and smiled.

Blythe managed a small smile. A polite smile. The kind of smile that came with effort and a certain degree of reluctance. 'Hello,' she said.

There was an awkward pause and Madison tried to think of something to say. 'You're very brown,' she said, and then felt stupid for stating the obvious. The girl had been in the sun all afternoon.

'I don't suppose you tan, do you?' Blythe replied.

'No, I just go red like a lobster.'

Blythe screwed up her perfect nose in distaste. 'Like Robert,' she said. 'He just sweats and fries.'

Madison didn't think that was kind. 'Well, we've both got fair skin that burns easily,' she agreed. They wandered towards the terrace. As Blythe made no effort to make conversation, Madison felt obliged to. 'How long have you and Jack been together?' Madison asked.

'Six years,' Blythe replied, growing a little more lively. 'Everyone always asks us when we're going to get married. It's very tedious. We're as good as, you know.'

'I wasn't going to ask, actually,' said Madison.

Blythe stopped at the door to the terrace. 'Jack has had a hard time accepting that his father had an affair, you know, so you being here isn't easy for him.' She gave a little sniff. 'I'm just saying.'

Madison was taken aback by the hostile look in her eyes. 'I understand. I'm sure it's been a challenging time for all the family,' she said.

Blythe pulled a face. 'Hal thinks it's a joke and Arthur is so laid-back he doesn't care. Jack is very sensitive and has been the most challenged. He didn't want you to come. But you're here, so ...' She shrugged. 'He's making the best of a difficult situation.'

Madison didn't think it was Blythe's place to tell her this. 'Well, he's been very welcoming,' she said. 'I'm sure he knows that it's been challenging for me too.' By the look on Blythe's face, that was something that hadn't crossed her mind.

Dinner was pleasant beneath the vine. Candles glowed through the dusk and Robert filled everyone's glass, aware that a little alcohol would loosen their English reserve and help the conversation flow more easily.

Blythe barely touched her wine. She sat beside Jack and every time the conversation centred on Madison, she drew him away by talking to him in a low voice so that he had to lean towards her to hear. Madison didn't know whether she did it in order to support him, or to purposely obstruct his chances of getting to know his new sister.

Elizabeth tried to lure her eldest back into the

conversation, but Blythe had the upper hand. She was sitting next to him and succeeded in having a private chat, just the two of them. Madison was sitting between Robert and Hal. Robert gave her confidence, encouraging her to tell the funny stories she'd told him over their many lunches in London. Hal and Arthur laughed loudly and with some surprise, for neither had thought on meeting her that afternoon that she would be such a character. Every now and then Jack turned his attention towards the laughter, only to be swiftly pulled back into Blythe's clutches.

Elizabeth gave up trying to include him and enjoyed talking to Madison. She had been generous in agreeing to meet her and inviting her to Villa Aurora. However, her amusement at Robert's daughter was not at all generous, but genuine. She was as surprised as her two sons at how very likeable Madison was. The relief was so great that she drank twice as much wine as she would normally. When she went upstairs the world was spinning, so she changed into her nightie and crawled beneath the sheets without washing her face or brushing her teeth. Something she had never done in all her married years.

'It's going well, isn't it?' said Robert, climbing into bed beside her.

'Very,' she mumbled, sinking slowly into sleep.

'Thank you, darling. I owe you everything. I could not have a more selfless wife. Really, I can't think of another woman who would have behaved with your graciousness and kindness and your downright goodness. I'm so lucky to have married you.'

He waited for Elizabeth to reply. When she didn't, he realised he would have to save his speech for another time. She had already fallen asleep. 'Night-night, darling one,' he said, and patted her gently on the arm.

Madison stayed up with Hal and Arthur, playing cards. Blythe said she was tired and persuaded Jack to go with her to their room. Madison sensed he would have preferred to play cards. His face had lit up when Hal had gone to get them and he'd looked disappointed when Blythe had said she didn't want to play. Hal poured more wine. Arthur lit a cigarette. Madison shuffled the cards. By the time they finished, it was two in the morning and all the candles had burned down to the end of their wicks.

Madison went to bed feeling happy. Her fears about meeting her half-brothers and Elizabeth had melted away. She was left with a warm feeling of having been welcomed into the family. She didn't consider Jack. He and Blythe had separated themselves from the group. Madison had let them go without regret. She hadn't expected any of them to like her, so the fact that most of them did was a bonus. She could live without Jack's affection.

The following morning Madison woke early. In spite of a mild headache, she was excited. The sun was streaming in through the thin linen curtains. Birds twittered in the trees and a light breeze brought in the sweet scents of honeysuckle and lavender. She wanted to enjoy every moment of being here, which meant not wasting it by lying in bed.

She slipped into a pair of denim shorts and a t-shirt and found Elizabeth at the breakfast table. An elderly lady in a long black dress was putting bowls of fruit and plates of croissants on the table alongside a jug of fresh orange juice and an array of jams and yogurts.

'Morning, Madison,' said Elizabeth, taking off her glasses and putting down her pen. Madison noticed she was writing a shopping list. 'You're up early.'

'I don't want to miss a minute of being in this beautiful place,' Madison replied.

'This is Signora Benotti,' said Elizabeth. 'She doesn't speak a word of English.' Signora Benotti heard her name and smiled shyly at Madison, who smiled back.

'I'm afraid I don't speak a word of Italian,' said Madison.

'It doesn't matter,' said Elizabeth. 'A smile says more than a thousand words.'

Madison liked Elizabeth. She was gentle and warm but had a directness that appealed to her. She was the sort of woman who called a spade a spade, unlike Madison's mother, who was tricky and never said what she really thought. You had to work it out from her mood or the expression on her face. Elizabeth, on the other hand, seemed to be a woman who said what she thought firmly and decisively, which Madison found refreshing.

The two women chatted as Madison ate a croissant and sipped a glass of orange juice. Everything tasted better in Italy.

Not long after, Blythe and Jack emerged. Blythe looked immaculate in a white sundress, her dark hair pulled back into a ponytail. Her skin was glossy and flawless. Jack was in a pair of shorts and a loose shirt. Neither looked particularly happy.

Madison wondered whether they had had a row, or whether Jack was simply hungover. They mumbled a good morning and then sat at the table. Signora Benotti brought them cups of coffee. Jack ate heartily while Blythe ate nothing. Madison didn't imagine she kept a figure like that by eating croissants.

Elizabeth looked at Blythe. 'Would you be sweet and nip to the shop?' she asked her.

Blythe didn't look too pleased. 'Sure. Jack and I can go after breakfast.'

'Actually, I need Jack. You can go on your own. Take my car. Here's the list.'

Blythe was left no choice. She looked at Jack, but Jack didn't argue with his mother. In fact, as he buttered another croissant, he began to cheer up.

Chapter 9

Giovanni's vineyard

Once Blythe had disappeared down the drive in Elizabeth's car, Elizabeth turned to Jack. 'Darling, I wonder whether you would do me a favour. I need a letter delivered to Giovanni. Perhaps you could take it this morning. Madison can go with you. It will be a nice way of showing her a bit more of Tuscany. She can take my bicycle.'

Jack grinned. 'You could have given it to Blythe,' he said.

'I didn't want to give it to Blythe,' Elizabeth replied crisply. 'It's an important letter and I want *you* to deliver it.'

He looked at Madison. 'I take it you can ride a bike?'

'Oh yes, that's a gene I've inherited from the Seymours.'

He laughed. 'I had to check. You never know.'

'I might not be able to play tennis, Jack, but

I'm a fiend behind the handlebars.' Madison got up from the table. 'Shall we head off, then?'

Elizabeth gave Jack the letter, which he put into his shirt pocket, and watched them set off down the drive on their bicycles.

Madison loved the feeling of free-wheeling down the hill, cruising over the shadows the cypress trees threw across the track, with the wind in her hair and the smell of wild herbs in her nostrils. She breathed it all in happily. Jack led the way until they reached the road at the bottom and then they were able to cycle side by side.

'You're so lucky to live in this paradise,' she said, taking in the pretty farmhouses.

'Dad bought the villa when I was a boy, so we've spent every summer here for as long as I can remember.'

'Do you know, this is my first trip to Italy?'

'No!' He looked at her in disbelief.

'Really. I've never been to Rome or Florence.'

'You'd love Florence.'

'I know. I'll get there one day. This has given me a taste of Italy. I now want more.'

He smiled. 'You know, we could go. It's a couple of hours' drive but I'd be happy to take you. You can't come to Tuscany and not visit Florence. I would feel that, as your brother, I would have failed you.'

She laughed. 'Then, as your sister, I'd love to take you up on your offer. I'm not sure Blythe will let you go, though.'

'It'll be a challenge, for sure. She's been loads of times and I don't imagine she'll want to go again.'

'Listen, if it's difficult, perhaps Robert can take me.'

'We could go together. Make a day of it.'

'That would be amazing.'

'Consider it done,' he said firmly. But Madison secretly doubted he would get it past Blythe.

A few minutes later they turned off the road and walked their bikes slowly up a dirt track that cut between two fields of vines. They ambled in silence, enjoying the peace and catching their breath. Then Jack looked at her steadily. 'Can I ask you some personal questions?' he said.

'Sure,' she replied.

'When did your mother tell you that your stepfather was not your real father?'

'I can't remember. I've always known that Tom wasn't my real father. She must have told me when I was very small because I grew up knowing that my real father was someone else.'

'Did she say who he was?'

'No, she said she would tell me on my eighteenth birthday.'

'She never told you his name? Not even his first name?'

'No. I knew he was paying for me, because she always told me how generous he was. You know, she'd say, "You can thank your father for this," when she bought my school uniform or a new winter coat. I knew he knew who *I* was, and that was nice.'

Jack frowned. 'Did you wonder about him? About what sort of man he was?'

Madison smiled sheepishly. 'All the time. I looked in the mirror every day and tried to find his features in mine, because I don't look like my mother at all.'

'That must have been hard.'

She shrugged. 'I suppose it was, but I was used to it. It's the way it was. Of course, I wanted to be like everyone else and have a father. I mean, I *did* have a father. Tom was my father, but everyone knew he wasn't my *real* father. At school I was a bit of a curiosity. My friends teased me – not unkindly. They thought he might be a famous movie star or something, because he'd met Mum in New York. I always knew I was named after the street where I was conceived.' She laughed. 'It's absurd, isn't it, to call your child after a street?'

'I think Madison's a nice name.'

'Thank you.'

Jack paused a moment, reflecting on her words. 'You've been brave,' he said.

'Have I?'

'Yes, very.'

'I just wanted to know who he was. I'm sorry if it was hard for you and your brothers, and your mother of course. I'm sorry about that.'

'It was hard, but now I've met you I feel better about it. I'm sure Hal and Arthur feel the same. Mum's been amazing. Dad doesn't deserve her.'

'There are no bad guys,' said Madison. 'Everyone's just trying to do the right thing.'

Jack looked doubtful. 'I think we can probably agree that Dad's the bad guy,' he said.

'Well, yes, I suppose he didn't cover himself in glory, did he? But if he hadn't been bad, I wouldn't be here, and I'm so happy that I *am* here.'

Jack grinned at her. 'I'm happy you're here too, Madison. Although, I'm happy to admit that you're a lot less like a Seymour than I thought you'd be.'

'Is that a compliment?'

'It is. You bring something different to the family, and that's a good thing.'

They arrived at a farmhouse sheltered beneath a canopy of umbrella pines. 'Giovanni looks after the villa while Mum and Dad are in England,'

Jack told her, leaning his bike against a wall. 'He's a real character. Come, I'll introduce you.'

A moment later a grey-haired man wandered out of a barn. He saw Jack and waved. '*Buon giorno*,' he exclaimed, his old face opening into a smile. 'And who is this *bellissima donna*?'

'This is my half-sister, Madison,' said Jack. Madison enjoyed the warm feeling of being introduced as a member of the family. She shook Giovanni's hand.

'You have a sister suddenly?' he exclaimed. 'Did an angel drop her from heaven or did she step out of a rose?'

Madison laughed.

'An angel dropping her from heaven is a nice way of putting it,' said Jack. He took the letter out of his pocket. 'Mum wanted me to give you this. She says it's important.'

Giovanni frowned. He opened the letter and read it. Then he chuckled and folded it away. 'Stay for a drink. Pretty girls dropped to earth by angels are very rare. My garden attracts beautiful creatures. Last night a little deer came to eat my grass. Come, perhaps we will see him again.'

They walked round the house to the garden where a table and chairs were arranged beneath a fig tree with a stunning view of the vineyard. Giovanni went inside to fetch the drinks. He tossed the letter into the bin. It had been a simple message written in Italian:

Please entertain Jack and Madison for a while – keep them for as long as you can, preferably until lunch! Thank you. Elizabeth

Chapter 10

Florence

Jack and Madison stayed with Giovanni until well after midday. Giovanni insisted on showing Madison the vineyard, the grape presses and the cellars where he kept the barrels. Jack had seen it all before, but he wandered around happily with his hands in his pockets. He was enjoying Madison's company and the high-spirited Giovanni, who convinced them to stay every time Jack looked at his watch and suggested they start cycling home.

When they eventually arrived back at the villa, Blythe was in a bate. 'You've been hours,' she grumbled from her sun lounger. 'What happened? Did you get lost?'

'Giovanni wanted to show Madison around the vineyard,' Jack explained, unbuttoning his shirt and stepping out of his shoes. 'Are you going to come in for a swim?' he asked Madison, before diving into the water.

Madison changed into her swimsuit. She was

self-conscious even though Jack, Hal and Arthur were in fact her brothers. So she wrapped a towel around her waist before emerging from the changing room.

'It's so refreshing!' Jack shouted from the pool, setting off for a lap of front crawl. Hal and Arthur got off their loungers and approached. As Madison padded across the hot stones to the shallow end, Blythe got into the pool. With slow, lazy strides she moved her perfect body towards the water. Madison tossed her towel to the side and jumped in.

It was lovely to be in the cool water. Madison swam some lengths, answering questions from Arthur and Hal about her visit to Giovanni's vineyard. When she and Jack laughed about Giovanni calling her an angel dropped from heaven, Blythe swam over to Jack and put her arms around him as if she owned him. She tickled his ribs and bit his ear and he laughed, although his face betrayed a slight irritation at being drawn away from the general conversation.

Madison wondered why Blythe minded so much. It wasn't as if Madison was going to steal Jack away. He was her blood. It simply wasn't an option.

After a delicious lunch, everyone disappeared inside for siestas. The heat of the day was heavy and sapped them of energy. Elizabeth showed Madison the library, which was a sitting room with wall-to-wall books. 'There are some wonderful novels here, if you'd like something to read.'

Madison chose a novel and took it into the garden and sat in the shade to read it. She had read a few chapters when Jack flopped down on the bench opposite. 'Hello,' she said, taking her eyes off the page.

'I've talked to Dad about Florence and he thinks it's a great idea.'

'Really? You can come?'

He pulled a face like a schoolboy who knows he's in trouble, but is going to continue being naughty all the same. 'Blythe's not happy about it, but I'm going anyway. I tried to persuade her to join us, but she says she's bored of Florence.'

Madison couldn't imagine how anyone could be bored of Florence. 'Lucky her to have been so many times,' she said.

'Her modelling takes her all over the world. I think she's even bored of Milan, Paris and Rome.'

Madison laughed. 'What isn't she bored of?'

He grinned. 'Me, *yet.*'

'I think you're safe there. I don't think she's ever going to be bored of *you.*'

*

That evening Blythe complained of a headache and insisted that Jack accompany her once again to their bedroom just as Hal pulled out his playing cards for a game of poker. Madison stayed at the table with her father, Hal and Arthur.

Elizabeth watched them play, with a full glass of wine and a contented smile on her face. *So this is what it would be like to have a daughter*, she thought, enjoying the sight of the four of them getting along so well. It was just a shame that Jack had gone to bed. She had rather hoped he would leave Blythe to go on her own. She sipped her wine, felt her whole body loosen as if her bones were made of dough, and decided that she really didn't like Blythe at all. Jack needed to find a nice girl like Madison.

Later, when Elizabeth and Robert climbed into bed, Robert drew her into his arms. 'You're an incredible woman, darling,' he said, kissing her temple. 'I'm so lucky to have you. Not only are you beautiful and clever and kind, but you're wise. Wiser than I'll ever be. I really love and appreciate you.'

Elizabeth's heart swelled with happiness. 'I forgive you, Robert,' she replied softly.

Robert never thought he'd hear her say that. 'Oh, Elizabeth, I . . .'

Elizabeth silenced him with a kiss. She propped

herself up on her elbow and looked at him tenderly. 'Every black cloud has a silver lining, and Madison is just that. A silver lining. I'm glad she's in our life.'

'I'm glad *I'm* still in your life,' said Robert, feeling very lucky.

Elizabeth nuzzled him. 'So am I,' she whispered.

The following day Robert, Jack and Madison drove to Florence. The sun was bright in a cornflower blue sky. Below it the Tuscan hills shimmered in the heat. Robert's car was big and comfortable, and they chatted all the way. Madison felt at ease with Robert and Jack, and by the time they reached Florence they were the best of friends.

Madison had seen Florence in movies and books, but the sight and feel of it was a completely different experience. They wandered around the ancient streets and squares, over paving stones worn by centuries of footsteps, and took in the splendours of this enchanting city.

Jack was pleased that Madison was so visibly impressed. Blythe was never impressed with anything unless it was a new handbag or a piece of jewellery. When the heat got too much, Jack bought Madison a straw hat from a little boutique down a shady alleyway. He insisted they eat ice creams beside a fountain to cool down. Most of all they laughed. They laughed a lot.

Robert had booked a table in his favourite restaurant, and they ate pasta and drank wine outside, watching the tourists and locals ambling slowly across the square. 'Thank you for bringing me here,' said Madison, as the waiter placed a large slice of tiramisu in front of her. 'This is now my favourite city in the world.'

'I agree,' said Robert. 'Florence is certainly in my top five.'

'Wait till you see Rome,' said Jack, watching her closely.

'Yes,' said Robert eagerly. 'You'll have to come back.'

Madison smiled. She didn't think she'd ever felt so happy, 'I'd love to,' she replied.

'Don't you dare visit Rome without me,' said Jack. The way he looked at her made something inside her stomach flip over. She averted her eyes and lifted her wine glass. He was her brother, she reminded herself. But she couldn't deny that she was beginning to find him attractive.

After lunch they wandered along the River Arno, admiring the famous bridge, the Ponte Vecchio. Madison was moved by the way Robert and Jack had treated her, as if she was special. When, as a little girl growing up, she had imagined her father, she had never imagined him to be as wonderful as Robert. She had never even thought about siblings, either, and now she had not only found her father, but had three big brothers too.

Jack made her feel protected. He walked on the outside of the pavement, opened doors for her and looked out for her when they were in a crowd. Madison had never experienced that before. She walked beside him and felt proud. *He's my brother*, she kept telling herself. Yet beneath her happiness a shadow of anxiety was forming that hadn't been there before. She couldn't allow herself to fall in love with her brother.

They were quiet on the drive back to the villa. Jack dozed in the front seat. Madison gazed out of the window, watching the sky turn to indigo blue and the first stars twinkling through it. She felt a deep contentment and yet, at the same time, a strange sadness. The day was ending. It had been perfect. She did not want to start a new one, especially as Blythe would be in it.

Chapter 11

A game of tennis

It was on the fifth day that Madison began to get the impression that Jack's feelings for her were becoming less fraternal and edging into something more romantic. She was sitting on the bench with Elizabeth, watching Jack and Arthur play tennis against Robert and Hal. It was a close match and all four men were excellent players. Blythe had joined them for half an hour but then left, claiming she needed to drive into town to buy something at the pharmacy.

Madison and Elizabeth chatted quietly, clapping dutifully every time someone played a good shot or served an ace. When it finished, with Robert and Hal having won by a whisker, Jack asked Madison if she wanted to knock a ball about with him.

'I'm hardly dressed for tennis,' she said.

'This isn't Wimbledon,' he replied.

She followed him onto the court. 'I'm really bad,' she warned him.

'I don't care. It'll be fun. Come on.' He handed her Hal's racket.

The others went off to swim and Elizabeth returned to her gardening. Jack patted a ball at Madison, who managed to pat it back. 'I thought you said you couldn't play!' he laughed.

Madison ran for the next ball and missed it. 'You see. The first was a fluke.'

'Do you want some constructive advice?'

'Sure, but it'll take one hell of a coach to improve my game.'

'That's me. One hell of a coach,' he said with a wink. He walked round to her side of the court and showed her how to hold her racket correctly. As he took her hand and placed it on the grip, she felt a frisson. She looked into his eyes and tried not to reveal the unexpected feelings his touch had given her. *He's my brother*, she kept telling herself, and yet, how could she feel sisterly towards him when they were adults who had only just met?

He dropped a ball and taught her how to bring her racket back and brush up the back of it in a top spin. As her shots grew stronger, his smile grew wider. 'You see,' he said. 'One hell of a coach.'

They played for half an hour and Madison

realised that she wasn't as hopeless as she had thought. She simply lacked coaching and practice. They were sitting on the grass drinking lemonade and chatting when Blythe appeared, looking furious. 'Here you are!' she said, and put her hands on her hips. 'I thought you said you didn't play tennis,' she added to Madison, her voice mildly accusing, as if Madison had somehow deceived her.

'Turns out I'm a Seymour, after all,' Madison replied, and Jack laughed.

Blythe didn't. 'Tea is on the terrace,' she said. 'Signora Benotti has baked a lemon cake. Are you going to come?'

Jack knew that wasn't a question but a command. 'Sure,' he said, getting up. 'I can't say no to Signora Benotti's cake.' Nor to Blythe, it seemed. He turned to Madison. 'We'll play a game next time.'

That evening, as Madison was going to her room to change for dinner, she heard raised voices in the room down the corridor. She hovered on the landing, curious to hear what the row was about. It became apparent very quickly that it was about *her*.

'You spend all your time with her,' Blythe was complaining.

'She's my sister.'

'Half.'

'The whole point of inviting her out here was to get to know her. How can I get to know her if I don't spend time with her?'

'But you're ignoring *me*!'

Madison didn't want to be caught loitering and hurried into her room, closing the door softly behind her. Her heart was pounding. But it was true. Since Florence, Jack had spent more time with her than he had with Blythe. They had so much to talk about. Like his father, he enjoyed books and art and films, and he seemed to want to talk about those things.

It was as if he'd been denied those kinds of conversations with Blythe. But most of the time they talked about nothing. They just talked. Madison liked being with him and, she now realised, Jack liked being with her too. *He's my brother,* she told herself again. Over and over. *He's my brother. Don't forget yourself.*

Blythe did not come down for dinner. Instead, she ate cheese and crackers in her room. No one mentioned her at the table. Madison wondered whether she had sulked like this before, because everyone seemed to accept her absence as normal and carried on as if nothing were wrong. It was only after dinner when Hal, Arthur, Robert and Elizabeth played a complicated word game that

Madison had never played before, that Jack told her what had happened.

They took a bottle and their glasses of rosé and sat on a swing chair at the other end of the terrace. Madison settled into the corner and sat cross-legged, while Jack lay back against the cushions. 'I'm in real trouble,' he told her.

'I think we all know that. The walls aren't very thick.'

'Blythe's furious with me for spending time with you,' he said.

Madison tried to be diplomatic. 'Well, I can understand her resentment. I mean, this is your holiday together as well as time to get to know me. She's just feeling unloved.'

'She's jealous.'

'She needn't be. I'm your half-sister.'

'I know. But you make her feel less-than.'

Madison was astonished. 'How can I make her feel less-than? She's a model. She's beautiful.'

Jack looked at her and frowned. 'Beauty's only skin deep, Madison. You know that.'

'Sure, but she's confident and elegant ...'

'But you're funny.' He turned his eyes away and sipped his wine. A sense of humour was certainly something Blythe didn't have.

'She doesn't need to be funny, because you're funny, so you can make her laugh.'

He nodded, but she could tell he didn't agree with her.

'She just needs reassurance and she'll be fine. Take her off somewhere tomorrow. There must be a town near here with some nice shops.'

'I don't want to leave the villa.'

'Why? You took me to Florence.'

He smiled and shook his head, as if he could see things very clearly that Madison could not. 'That's different.'

'Not really. For someone who doesn't want to leave the villa, Florence is a hell of long way away.'

He drained his glass. 'I don't want to leave the villa, Madison, because *you're* here.'

'Oh, I see,' she said and laughed, making light of something growing suddenly heavy.

'I'm serious. I'm enjoying being with you.' Then, as if aware of how wrong that sounded, he added quickly, 'I've never had a sister before.'

'I've never had an older brother. Now I have three,' she said and laughed again. There followed a long pause. They both stared into their glasses.

'Shame you're my sister,' he said after a while, and looked her dead in the eye.

'Don't say it,' she whispered. Her heart thumped.

He shrugged. 'Why not? It's of no consequence. You're Dad's daughter.'

'Because tomorrow, when you're sober, you'll wish you hadn't.'

'I'm sober now.'

'You'll still wish you hadn't. And you'll feel bad that you did, because of Blythe.'

'Maybe Blythe is right to throw a tantrum. Perhaps she can sense something in the air.'

'I think I should go to bed,' said Madison.

'Don't go to bed yet. I'm sorry. Let's talk about something else.'

'You're going to have to face Blythe sometime, you know,' she said and smiled.

'Not yet. The night is young. Let's have another drink.' Jack picked the bottle up from the ground and refilled their glasses. 'You haven't told me about your romantic life.'

'There's not much to tell.'

'Then spin it out, because I'm enjoying your company and I don't want the night to end.'

Chapter 12

The midnight swim

Madison and Jack talked until three in the morning. They finished their bottle of wine and opened another one. Then, unsteady on their feet and clinging to each other for balance, they headed down to the pool to go for a 'midnight swim'. Everyone else had gone to bed. The garden was quiet but for the gentle chirruping of crickets. Above them the stars shone, and the moon, like a giant silver crystal, seemed bigger and brighter than ever.

They stripped off and dived into the water naked. Madison was aware that she was drunk, but, being drunk, she didn't care. They were laughing at nothing and everything, the frisson between them now enhanced by the wine and the moon, which cast an unearthly glow upon the water. They splashed about, circling each other until the circle became smaller and they found themselves at the edge of the pool, staring into each other's eyes and finding only willingness and desire there.

'I want to kiss you,' said Jack suddenly.

Madison wanted him to kiss her too, but the sensible voice of reason, previously dulled by alcohol, now made itself heard.

'I want you to,' she said. 'But we can't. We're brother and sister.'

'Are you sure?' he replied. 'We don't look anything alike. In fact, you don't really look like Dad at all. You just have blue eyes and fair hair.' He touched her face. 'You're very pretty, you know.'

She gently removed his hand. 'You have a girlfriend,' she reminded him. 'You're going to be in a lot of trouble.'

'What if I just try it out? If it feels weird, I'll stop.'

Madison giggled. 'It won't feel weird. I barely know you.'

'Perhaps it's a mistake and you're not really my sister at all. Anyway, you're only half. Does that make a difference?' He pulled a face, which made Madison laugh again.

'I think it does, Jack. Blood is blood.'

'I wish you weren't my blood.'

'I wish you weren't my blood too.'

'And that's not the wine talking. I really

mean it. You make me feel good. I like being with you.'

'I like being with you as well.' She wished he'd put his arms around her. She edged away, so he couldn't. 'But we're playing with fire. I think we should get out.'

'And lie under the stars to dry off.'

Madison climbed out and grabbed a towel. She chucked one at him. He wrapped it around his waist. 'Come on,' he said, taking her hand. 'Let's go and lie under the stars.'

They lay on a pair of sun loungers, staring into the sky. It really was incredibly beautiful. Madison sighed with both pleasure and regret. Out of all the men in the world, the one she liked was one she could never have. It seemed cruel of fate to have made it so.

'I was furious with Dad for having been unfaithful to Mum, but now I understand. If you weren't my sister, I'd be unfaithful to Blythe, right now, right here, with Blythe in the house. That makes me a real cad,' he said. 'I'm just as bad as Dad.'

'But you've done nothing wrong,' Madison reassured him.

They lay in silence for a while, allowing the beauty of the night to surround them. Eventually, Jack turned to her. 'Are you going to be embarrassed tomorrow morning?' he said. 'I mean, we're both drunk. Are you going to regret this when you're sober?'

'It's almost dawn already. Look, you can see the glow over there.' Madison pointed to the horizon where a faint blush could be seen shining through the darkness. 'I'm not regretting it yet.'

'That's because you're still drunk. How will I know you don't regret it? Will you give me a sign?'

'I can do better than that,' she said. 'I'll slip you a note.'

'What will it say?'

'I don't know. I haven't thought about that yet. But I'll slip you a note to say that I don't regret swimming naked with you in the middle of the night. Nor the things we said to one another. The wine just made it possible for those things to come out. They were already there.'

'We're going to have to be friends, Madison.' Jack sighed.

'I know.'

'Do you think we can do it?'

'If we try hard enough, we can do anything.'

'Maybe I'll stop fancying you.' He looked at her and grinned.

'I'm sure you will. I'll probably stop fancying you too.' They laughed again.

His face grew serious, suddenly. 'I hope I do, because I don't want to go through my whole life fancying you and not being able to have you. That would be torture.' He took her hand then and brought it to his lips. 'This will have to do,' he said. 'A chaste kiss on your hand.'

It was five in the morning when they walked back up to the house. Neither wanted the night to end. They stopped at the door to the villa, and Jack pulled Madison into his arms. He pressed his lips against her temple. 'I think someone up there is having a laugh at our expense,' he said.

She hugged him back, resting her head against his chest. 'I think you're right. When I discovered I had three half-brothers, I never expected to be attracted to one of them.'

'It's the kind of thing movies are made of.'

'One for your father, then.'

'He's your father too.'

'Unfortunately.' Aware that that sounded ungrateful, she added quickly. 'You know what I mean.'

He pulled away and smiled down at her wearily. 'I most certainly do.'

Madison climbed into bed and wondered whether Jack had been able to sneak into his bedroom without waking Blythe. She curled into a ball and hugged her pillow. Closing her eyes, it was Jack's face that she saw. Jack's face that stayed there when she tried to think of something else. She sighed and willed herself to sleep. What would the morning bring, she wondered? Perhaps it would have been better if she hadn't come to Italy after all.

Madison was woken by the sound of voices on the terrace below. She could hear Hal's dry humour and husky laugh rising above the others. The clinking of cutlery and smell of coffee wafted into her bedroom and she realised that it was breakfast.

She looked at her watch. It was nine am. She'd slept about three and a half hours at the most. She closed her eyes and groaned. The night before was fresh in her memory. Contrary to what Jack had said, she was not embarrassed by what had occurred. She was a little sad, but relieved, by what hadn't.

She rolled on to her back and blinked in the bright sunlight. There was no dilemma. There was no 'what should I do?' because there was only one thing she *could* do; pretend that she didn't fancy him. He was her brother and that was an unchangeable fact. No amount of wishing or longing would change their relationship. She had to find a way to be a sister to him, or she wouldn't be able to see him at all.

Eventually, Madison got up and showered. She wondered how much the rest of the family knew. Did they know she and Jack had gone swimming in the middle of the night? Did they know that they'd talked until dawn? Had they guessed that there was an attraction between them? Would Elizabeth sense it and not want to see her again? What would Robert think?

Finally, Madison summoned her courage and went downstairs. She glanced at Jack's door and wondered what was going on behind it. Was he in terrible trouble? Madison felt hungover and tired, but adrenalin had kicked in and made her alert. It was daunting stepping out onto the terrace, but she lifted her chin and decided she would be cheerful and breezy, as she always was. She would act as if nothing unusual had gone on in the moonlight.

'Ah, Madison,' said Robert, smiling over his glass of orange juice.

'What time did *you* get to bed?' Hal asked, looking her over with an amused expression on his face.

'Must have been late. You and Jack were deep in conversation when I went to bed at one,' Arthur added.

'I don't know,' Madison replied with a smile. 'I think it was very late. We went for a swim.' She laughed as if she thought the idea mad. 'It was fun, swimming beneath the stars.'

'You must have been drunk,' said Hal.

'I think I was.' Madison realised that it was better to hide in plain sight than to pretend they'd gone to bed shortly after everyone else. A lie was always more believable if it was a half-truth.

'Come and have something to eat,' said Elizabeth, and Madison realised from her smile that she had no idea how close her eldest son had come to kissing his new half-sister.

Madison sat down and poured herself a cup of coffee. She didn't feel like eating, but she knew from experience that a little food would make her feel better. She buttered a croissant and spread a thick layer of jam before taking a bite. The taste alone chased away her headache.

'What on earth did you and Jack talk about for so long?' asked Arthur. Madison thought she noticed an edge of jealousy to his voice.

Madison shrugged. 'I don't know. I think it was the wine talking. I have very little memory of last night at all. Except that it was fun. You should have joined us, Arthur. You too, Hal. Next time I make a rash decision to swim in the middle of the night, I'll come and drag you both out of bed.'

They laughed. Arthur seemed satisfied. Hal made a joke, but before Madison had the chance to fire one back at him, Blythe and Jack stepped out of the French doors. Madison was eager to read their body language. To her surprise, Blythe was in a good mood. She looked beautiful in a scarlet dress with white flowers embroidered on it, a straw hat and sunglasses. Her hair was tied into a plait. Jack said 'good morning' and plonked himself into a chair. Blythe sat beside him and reached for the orange juice. She poured them both a glass.

'Jack and I are going to Rome,' she announced, her face radiant with pleasure.

'What? Today?' said Robert in surprise.

'We thought we'd go for a couple of nights,' said Jack. He didn't catch Madison's eye, but swept his gaze evenly over the family.

'Oh,' said Elizabeth, put out. 'Madison will be leaving before you get back, then.'

Blythe looked at Madison and pretended to be sad. 'That's a shame. Still, it's been lovely spending these days getting to know you.'

'Yes, it has,' Jack agreed, glancing at Madison for a moment before turning back to his glass of orange juice.

Blythe smiled at Elizabeth. 'I'm excited to be going to Rome. It's the most romantic city in the world.' She took Jack's hand. 'I know I won't be disappointed.'

Chapter 13

The departure

Once Jack and Blythe had left, Madison felt as if the energy had been sucked out of the place. She felt strangely deflated. Jack had barely looked at her at breakfast, and it seemed as if the fun they had had the night before had never happened. He had said goodbye to her in front of the whole family, kissing her on her cheek and saying how nice it was that she had been able to come out and meet them all. 'I hope to see you back in the UK,' he had said before he and Blythe had left in a taxi bound for the airport.

It had been swift. Madison suspected that Blythe had come up with the idea only that morning and somehow bullied Jack to go along with it. Jack had told Madison that Blythe wasn't excited by Rome, so she wondered why the change of heart?

Once they had gone, Hal predicted that they

would be engaged by the time they returned to London. 'I hope not,' said Arthur with a grimace. 'I don't want Blythe as a sister-in-law.'

'Arthur!' said his mother, giving him a sharp look. 'That's not very kind.'

'If and when the time comes,' said Robert, putting his napkin on the table. 'We will welcome her into the family.'

'She's already in the family,' said Hal. 'Unfortunately.'

'What is it with you boys?' said Elizabeth.

Hal laughed. 'Don't pretend you like her, Mum. None of us like her but Jack.'

'And he's the only one who needs to like her,' Elizabeth replied firmly. 'If he is indeed going to marry her.'

'It's what Blythe wants,' added Arthur.

'What Blythe wants, Blythe gets,' said Hal.

Arthur looked at Madison, who was feeling low. 'Fancy cycling into town?' he asked.

'I'd love to,' she replied, recalling with a twinge of longing her cycle ride with Jack.

'I'll come too,' added Hal, getting up from the table. 'Then we can come back and enjoy a big lunch.'

'You'll have certainly earned it if you're going to cycle,' said Elizabeth.

Madison did not really feel like cycling. She

had no energy, but she got up and went to her bedroom to change into a pair of shorts. She closed the door and went to the window. Now Jack had gone, the Tuscan landscape had lost something of its splendour and charm. He was her brother, she reminded herself. She couldn't have him. But her heart wouldn't listen.

She slipped into shorts, t-shirt and trainers and made to leave. Just as she was about to open the door, something on her pillow caught her attention. It was an envelope. Her heart flared with hope. She opened it to find a white card which read:

I still want to kiss you ...

She sat down and took a deep breath. Jack must have written it just before leaving, which meant his cold goodbye was just an act. Madison stared at the note. He still wanted to kiss her. She still wanted to kiss *him*; but they could not.

When she cycled off with Arthur and Hal, she did so with a light spirit. It didn't matter that Jack wasn't there any more, because she knew he was thinking about her. He was thinking about her just as she was thinking about him. The fact that they couldn't ever be together no longer mattered, at least not right now. What mattered was that they *wanted* to be together. Madison was content with that.

The following day she packed her bag, said goodbye to Robert and Elizabeth and the boys, and climbed into the taxi to take her to the airport. It had been the most wonderful week of her life, and she had told Robert as much as he embraced her.

'We've all loved having you with us,' Robert had replied. 'You're a Seymour now. There will be no getting rid of us.' She had laughed and told him that she would never want that.

After Madison had left, Robert went off into the garden to sit in the shade and read. Yet he couldn't concentrate on the words. All he could think about was Madison and how incomplete the place now felt without her. He put down his book and let his gaze lose focus in the half-distance. Elizabeth was gardening. The boys were playing tennis. Jack was very likely proposing to Blythe. Robert didn't like Blythe, but he wasn't going to admit it. Perhaps, in time, they would come to like her, he thought. But he doubted it. She just didn't have the same values as they did.

After a while he was struck by an idea. A very good idea, too. He got up and went to find his wife. Elizabeth was dead-heading geraniums, putting the dry petals into a basket that she had hooked over her arm. 'Darling,' he began. 'I want to talk to you about something.'

She looked at him and smiled. 'It was a success, wasn't it?'

'Yes, it was.'

'I like her, you know. I was prepared not to, but I liked her the first moment I laid eyes on her.'

'I'm pleased.'

'It's nice for the boys to have a sister.'

'They seemed to like her too.'

'I'm sure we'll see more of her. At least, I hope we do. We must make an effort to include her in family get-togethers. I think she'd like that. She looked rather sad to be leaving, I thought.'

Robert seized upon this wave of enthusiasm that was carrying Elizabeth. 'I want to include her in my will,' he told her.

Elizabeth arched an eyebrow. 'I think that's a good idea.'

'Really? That's good. I'm glad you agree. I wouldn't want to do anything like that without your support.'

She laughed. 'Of course, I agree. It's the right thing to do.'

'Good.'

'Do me a favour, darling. Will you pass me the secateurs? I left them on the grass over there.'

That night as they were going to bed, Elizabeth put her magazine on the bedside table and took off her glasses. Robert, beside her, was reading his book. 'Darling,' she said. Her tone was such that Robert took his eyes off his book. It was the kind of tone she used when she was about to ask him something important.

'Yes?' he replied.

'About you changing your will and adding Madison ...'

'Yes?' he wondered whether she had changed her mind and was now *not* going to support him.

'Can I make a suggestion?'

'Of course.'

'Will you get a DNA test, just to make sure that Madison is, in fact, your daughter? Silly of me, I know. She so obviously is. But changing a will is a big deal. I think you should be sure.'

Robert was relieved. 'Of course, Elizabeth. It's a very wise suggestion. I should have thought of it myself.' He leant over and kissed her. 'You see, that's one of the reasons I married you. One of many. Thank you.'

*

A couple of days later Jack and Blythe returned to Villa Aurora. They had barely put their suitcases down before Elizabeth noticed the ring sparkling on Blythe's finger. She gasped. Blythe smiled proudly and held it out. 'We're engaged!' she squealed. 'Isn't it beautiful. It's diamonds and sapphires.'

Elizabeth swallowed. It was truly beautiful. 'Congratulations,' she said. She ought not to have been surprised, but the sight of that ring on Blythe's tapering finger gave her an uneasy feeling in her stomach.

The sound of Blythe squealing brought Hal, Arthur and Robert in from the terrace. They stood in the hall, admiring the ring and trying to pretend that they were all happy, as happy as Blythe. There was something in Jack's expression that caused the uneasy feeling in Elizabeth's stomach to intensify.

'Well done, Jack,' said Robert, patting his son on the back. 'Good choice.'

'Thanks, Dad.'

'Did he get down on one knee?' Hal asked.

'It was very romantic, wasn't it, Jack?' said Blythe, putting her arm around his waist. 'It was midnight and we were walking back to the hotel after dinner and he suddenly came out with it. Totally unexpected. He just took my hand and said, "Marry me, Blythe?" It would have been rude to have said no.' She laughed. 'We want to get married here.'

'Lovely,' said Elizabeth.

'When?' asked Robert.

'October,' said Blythe.

'That doesn't give you much time,' said Elizabeth.

'I've thought it all through,' said Blythe. 'Marriage in the church in town, dinner in the garden, dancing under the stars. It'll be so glamorous. We can't possibly get married in England. It's just so unimaginative. Jack and I want our day to be special and memorable.'

'Lovely,' Elizabeth repeated. Blythe really had thought it all through. Elizabeth rather resented her for not having asked, then felt bad for expecting her to. She and Jack had been a couple for six years. She already belonged here.

'Come on, Jack,' said Blythe, setting off up the stairs. 'I want to start writing the guest list.'

Chapter 14

The wedding

Madison was at her mother's house, sitting at the kitchen table reading the newspaper and trying not to think of Jack, when Robert telephoned. Alice was at the sink, loading the dishwasher. When Robert's voice came down the line, Madison was surprised. Robert had never called her at home before. She didn't imagine he wanted to speak to Alice.

'Robert,' said Madison.

'We miss you over here,' he said. 'The villa's not the same without you.'

'I miss you too. I had the most wonderful week.'

'You must come again next year. We'll make it an annual thing. It's a family holiday, after all, and you are family.'

'I'm very lucky.'

'No, we're the lucky ones. Listen, I need to talk to you about something important. I'd like to write you into my will.'

Madison was astonished. She caught her mother's eye. Alice had stopped what she was doing and was leaning against the sideboard, listening. Madison turned away. 'That's very generous of you, Robert,' she said, lowering her voice. Alice could still hear everything.

'You're my daughter so it's right that you should be included, along with the boys. One small thing, though, just a formality. I need you to have a DNA test.' He chuckled, clearly embarrassed to have to ask her. 'It's a bore, I know. But once it's done, it's done. Would you mind?'

'Of course not,' said Madison.

'I'll arrange it with my doctor. A simple blood test. Nothing sinister. And, by the way, Jack and Blythe are engaged.'

Madison felt as if she had been punched in the stomach. 'What?'

'Yes, wonderful news. Jack proposed in Rome. They're going to marry here at the villa.'

'When?'

'October.'

'Goodness, that's soon.'

'I know. Elizabeth is in a spin, as you can imagine. Blythe has grand plans.'

'It's wonderful news,' Madison said flatly. 'Please pass on my congratulations.'

'I will. You take care now. I'll be in touch as soon as I'm back in London at the beginning of September.'

When Madison hung up, her mother went to boil the kettle. 'Everything okay?' she asked.

'He's going to include me in his will.'

Alice spun around, a delighted look on her face. 'That's amazing. You know how rich he is, don't you?'

Madison shrugged. 'I suppose so. I hadn't really thought.'

'You'll get a lot of money.'

'I don't want his money, Mum. I'd rather have *him*.'

'Well, don't look so miserable about it. He's not dead yet.'

'No, he's not.' She drained her coffee cup. The coffee was cold. 'Jack's getting married. He's just got engaged to Blythe.'

'The one you don't like?'

'I don't think any of them really like her. She's not very likeable.'

'Jack must like her.'

Madison sighed. 'Yes, of course.' She stood up. 'I'm going for a walk.'

Alice smiled. 'Robert Seymour including you in his will. Who'd have thought it?' She shook her head. 'It's like winning the lottery.'

'Oh, Mum. That sounds terrible. His death will be nothing but loss for me, I can assure you.'

'He's always been generous. He did the right thing from the very beginning. I knew he would. You could tell he was a decent man just by looking at him. He had decent written all over his face.'

Madison hovered by the door. 'He wants me to have a DNA test,' she added. The gloomy tone in her voice had nothing to do with that, and everything to do with Jack and Blythe's engagement.

'What?' Alice screwed up her nose. But Madison was already outside, heading off towards the beach.

Madison reminded herself again that there was no point in wishing for Jack when there was no possibility of being able to have him. She tried to feel happy for him marrying Blythe, but she couldn't. The only man whom she had ever come close to loving was the one man she couldn't have. It seemed so unfair.

Madison marched up the beach. The waves rolled onto the shore leaving behind a beard of foam that quickly sank into the sand. Fat white clouds floated across the sky and the air was tangy with the scent of brine. It was beautiful. Madison stopped walking and gazed out to sea.

She thought of Jack. She pictured him in the pool, staring at her in the moonlight. *I want to kiss you*, he had said. She took a deep, jagged breath and cried into the wind.

Madison returned to London. Being busy kept her mind off Jack's impending wedding. It was ridiculous to mourn a man she barely knew. Ridiculous to care so much. Yet, she couldn't control the disappointment that lay like tar in the pit of her stomach.

Robert arranged the DNA test. Madison did as she was told and then thought nothing of it. Hal, who worked in Piccadilly, met her for lunch a couple of times and Arthur invited her to his birthday dinner at the Mirabelle restaurant in Mayfair. She hoped Jack would be there, but he wasn't. The invitation to his wedding arrived. Madison could barely look at it. She wrote a formal reply, knowing Elizabeth would expect that, then put it face down on the mantelpiece. It was going to be hard, attending the ceremony and party afterwards, pretending she was happy when she was quietly dying inside.

One evening after work, Jack telephoned. Madison was so stunned to hear his voice that she didn't know what to say. 'I need to talk to you, Madison. Can we meet?' He sounded down. Madison wondered with a flicker of hope whether he had called off his engagement.

'Of course,' she replied. 'When?'

'Now?'

Jack suggested a pub in Chelsea. Madison had no time to change. She was still in a pair of black trousers and a white shirt, having come straight from the office. She'd like to have at least had a shower and put on a pair of jeans. Jack was already at the bar. He looked serious until he saw her and then a smile lit up his face, and Madison's heart. They fell into an awkward embrace.

'You smell nice,' he said, looking into her face with his intense hazel eyes. Taking her all in. 'You look nice too.' He sighed. 'What do you want to drink?'

'Vodka, lime and soda, please,' she replied, barely believing that she was here with Jack. Jack, who she hadn't stopped thinking about since Italy.

They settled into a round corner table, away from the crowd. Jack took a swig of beer. 'Thank you for coming at such short notice,' he said.

'That's fine. I had nothing planned for tonight.'

He smiled and Madison was reminded of their midnight swim. He had smiled like that then, too. 'Congratulations,' she said. 'I received my invitation to the wedding.' She was about to carry on, about how lovely to get married in Italy, in the magnificence of Villa Aurora, but the words stuck in her throat. She took a sip of her drink.

He sighed. 'I'm doing the right thing,' he said. 'Blythe gave me an ultimatum. I didn't know what to do.' He looked at her steadily. 'You confused me, Madison.'

'I confused myself,' she replied.

'Did you find my note?'

'I thought *I* was meant to write one to *you*?'

'There wasn't time.'

'It was sweet. Thank you.'

'I meant it. I *still* mean it.'

Now Madison sighed. A heavy, hopeless sigh. 'You *are* doing the right thing,' she said firmly. 'We fancy each other now, but we'll get over it. You've been with Blythe for six years. You've known me one week. I'm sure, if you got to know me, I'd be very annoying. Or we would argue and disagree. Maybe if you did kiss me, we would have no chemistry. Perhaps the fact that we can't have each other makes us want each other more. I don't know. But you know Blythe, and you love her. We'll look back at our midnight swim and laugh about it one day.'

Jack took her hand and squeezed it. 'There, you see. You're not like anyone else. I can talk to you. Sure, I talk to Blythe, but it's not the same. With you, I feel you really see me. It's like there's no barrier. No separation. It's all a massive cliché, I know. I sound like an idiot. Perhaps love makes people idiotic. I needed to see you to tell you that I haven't stopped thinking about you since I left for Rome. And just because I'm getting married doesn't mean I'll stop thinking about you. But I have to try.'

'We're ridiculous, the two of us.'

He chuckled bitterly. 'We are. But you were right in Italy. We're half-siblings. We share the same blood. It's never going to be. So we have to accept that and make the best of it. At least you're going to be in my life.'

'That's a positive,' Madison said, trying to be upbeat when she really felt like crying.

'I figure that my marriage will prevent me from reaching for *you*.'

'That's never stopped anyone,' she laughed cynically.

He brought her hand to his lips. 'This is as close as I'll ever get,' he said. 'But it'll never be enough.'

Chapter 15

The Kiss

Madison packed for Italy. She had bought a new dress, but she felt no excitement at the thought of wearing it. She had been invited to stay at the villa with the family. Well, she was family, after all, she told herself. There was going to be a big dinner in the garden, and dancing. Hal had told her that the whole garden was going to be lit up with fairy lights and the villa itself would look magical. Blythe had elaborate ideas, but it was Elizabeth who was making it all happen.

The day before Madison was due to fly out, Robert appeared at her desk. He had a strange look on his face. 'Can I have a minute?' he said. Madison followed him into his office and closed the door. 'Sit down, Madison.' She did as she was told. For a moment she wondered whether he somehow knew about her and Jack and her stomach turned over. 'I'm afraid I've got some bad news.'

Madison noticed the strange look on his face

grow stranger still. 'The DNA result came back from the lab and …' he hesitated. 'I'm afraid, Madison, you're not my daughter after all.'

Madison stared at him in disbelief. 'Sorry?' she muttered. 'I don't understand.'

'You're not my daughter.' His eyes shone. He shook his head. 'I'm sorry. For you and for me.'

Madison's eyes filled with tears. 'Did my mother lie?' She put her head in her hands.

'I don't know. You'll have to ask her.' Robert walked to her side and put a hand on her shoulder. 'You might not be my daughter in blood, Madison, but you're my daughter in every other way,' he said softly. 'That won't change.'

But Madison knew it would.

'Why don't you take the rest of the day off?' he suggested.

She nodded and stood up. Robert pulled her into a hug. 'I'm as disappointed as you are,' he said, holding her tightly. 'But I haven't built a relationship with you only to end it today.' He smiled sympathetically. 'I'll see you in Italy?'

'I don't think I can go,' she said.

Robert looked as if he was about to try to persuade her, but thought better of it.

'It's going to take a while for this to settle in,' she explained.

'Of course,' he replied. 'You know, the boys

and Elizabeth will be as disappointed as I am. They rather took you to their hearts.'

'As I did,' said Madison. 'Thank you, Robert, for everything.'

As soon as Madison got home, she called her mother in tears.

'Hello, darling,' said Alice brightly.

'Why did you lie to me?' Madison asked. 'Robert isn't my father.'

There was a long pause. 'What are you talking about?' said Alice.

'I told you I was taking a DNA test and you said nothing.'

Another pause. Madison heard her mother sigh. 'I didn't know.'

'Yes, you did. Don't lie to me again. How many men were you sleeping with then?'

'That's unfair.'

'No, it isn't. You tell Robert that I'm his child and he pays handsomely for my upkeep for eighteen years. And you say nothing. Then you allow me to get in touch with him and he embraces me as his daughter. And you still say nothing? You let him pay. You let me meet him. You let us bond. You let me go to Italy and meet his wife and sons and still, you *say nothing*?'

'Madison, I was a young, unmarried woman. What was I to do?'

'Who is my father, then?'

Alice took a breath. 'I don't know. I had a brief fling with a bartender. I can't even remember his name. Robert was successful and rich. I knew he'd look after us.'

'What happened to the bartender?'

'I have no idea. I never saw him again.'

'So I'll never know who my father is?'

Alice sighed. 'In my day there was no such thing as a DNA test. You could have been Robert's or the bartender's. I took a gamble.'

'Well, there is a DNA test now and you've made me look like a fool.' Madison started to cry again. 'I loved him, Mum. I loved the whole family. I felt I belonged.'

'Madison, you have always belonged *here*. Tom has been more of a father to you than Robert could ever be. I didn't encourage you to look for your real father, because you already had one, one who loved you. But you wanted to pursue it and I supported you. Why are you craving another family when you *have* a family? We might not be rich and glamorous like the Seymours, but we love you. You're one of us.' Her voice softened. 'Yes, I lied. But I did it for *you*. Stop chasing rainbows and come home.'

Madison knew that, in spite of her mother's dishonesty, much of what she said was true. Madison already had a family who loved her. She had a father who was everything a father should be. Was blood so important? Did it really matter? Tom had always been there for her. Why had she not recognised that? 'I'll come home soon,' she said, suddenly feeling a swell of gratitude for Tom. 'Right now, I need to be alone. I need to work out what I'm going to do.'

Madison wasn't sure she would continue working for Robert. It would be awkward. She was also still living in the apartment he had bought for her. That wasn't right, either. She could never repay the money he had spent on her, but she could repay the money he had given her that she had saved.

As she looked over the apartment, she realised that it wasn't going to be possible to live in London any more either. She needed to get away. To start in a new place altogether. Perhaps she'd go to Milan, or Paris, or Madrid. She didn't think she could ever face the Seymours again. Least of all Elizabeth, who had probably been hurt the most by her husband's affair and yet had welcomed Madison into the family without any thought for herself.

Madison didn't think she could ever look *her* in the eye again.

The day of Jack's wedding came and went. Madison walked around Hyde Park, trying not to imagine him walking down the aisle and dancing beneath the stars with his new wife. How ironic it was that now they *could* be together, it was marriage, not blood, that would make it impossible. What a mess! But she needed to move on from him too, she realised. She needed to put the summer behind her. To try to forget that it ever happened.

The day after the wedding was a Sunday. Madison lay in bed, feeling miserable. Jack was now married. Hal and Arthur had no doubt danced until dawn. They might have even gone for a midnight swim. She could almost smell the garden. The scents of pine and rosemary and the sweet smell of jasmine that grew up the villa wall.

Her heart ached. She wished she were there. Even though she'd have had to watch Jack vow to love and cherish Blythe, she just wished she were still part of their family. A Seymour. But she was just Madison. Alone in London. Crying into her pillow.

She managed to drag herself out of bed at

midday and have a shower. She wished she were in Devon, then she could swim in the sea. She knew that would make her feel better, so she decided to take a train that afternoon and head home. She'd make it up with her mother and give Tom a massive hug. She turned the water to cold and breathed deeply as the icy water washed some of her unhappiness away.

The doorbell rang.

Wrapping herself in a towel, she went to answer it. She wondered who would come calling on a Sunday morning.

She opened the door. It was Jack.

Madison stared at him in astonishment. 'What are *you* doing here?' she asked.

'I've come to kiss you,' he said.

Before Madison could reply, he stepped into the apartment and pulled her into his arms, pressing his lips to hers in a passionate kiss. The questions in Madison's mind dissolved as she was overpowered by it. Jack kicked the door closed then buried his face in her neck. 'I heard the good news,' he murmured, edging her towards the bedroom. 'You're not my sister after all.'

'But you're married!' she exclaimed.

'No, I'm not. Dad was kind enough to tell me *before* the wedding. Blythe's furious and the guests arrived to find there was no wedding after all. I'm in terrible trouble. I know I've let Blythe down and I doubt she'll ever forgive me. But she is better off without me, she really is. And I suspect Mum and Dad are secretly relieved. They didn't like her. I got the first flight home, leaving all the guests having a fine old time.'

Madison's heart swelled with joy. 'You came back for *me*?'

'As soon as I could get away.' He unwrapped her towel. It fell at her feet. She stood naked before him. His hazel gaze looked deeply into hers and she recalled their midnight swim and the many others that they would have in the future. 'I don't think I've ever been so happy in all my life,' he said.

Madison laughed as they fell on to the bed. 'Nor me,' she agreed.

'I've wanted to kiss you, Madison, for so long, and now I can. All over. Every inch of you.' His lips hovered over hers. 'And I'm going to take it real slow.'

Acknowledgements

I would like to thank Fanny Blake for giving me the opportunity to write for Quick Reads and for her advice and direction, which was invaluable. Also, thank you to Louise Davies, Sian Wilson and David Reynolds. None of the Quick Reads would be possible without the brilliantly gifted writer Jojo Moyes, so I know I am not alone in showing my appreciation and gratitude. Thank you, Jojo!

Last but not least, thank you to my agent, Sheila Crowley, and my editor, Suzanne Baboneau, who are without question my Dream Team and more precious than gold!

It's been an absolute pleasure writing this story and I really hope my readers enjoy it.

Santa Montefiore

Stories that stay with you forever

Stay in touch with Santa for monthly updates
on her latest books.

Sign up for Santa's newsletter at
SantaMontefioreAuthor.com

You can also connect with Santa on social media,
or follow her on Amazon for new book alerts.

🐦 SantaMontefiore

📷 SantaMontefioreOfficial

f /SantaMontefiorebooks

a bit.ly/FollowSanta

THE
READING
AGENCY

About Quick Reads

*"Reading is such an important
building block for success"*

\- Jojo Moyes

Quick Reads are short books written by
best-selling authors. They are perfect for regular
readers and those who are still to discover the
pleasure of reading.

Did you enjoy this Quick Read?
Tell us what you thought by filling in
our short survey. Scan the QR code to
go directly to the survey or visit
https://bit.ly/QuickReads2022

Turn over to find your next Quick Read...

A special thank you to Jojo Moyes for her generous donation
and support of Quick Reads and to **Here Design**.

Quick Reads is part of The Reading Agency, a national charity
tackling life's big challenges through the proven power of reading.

www.readingagency.org.uk
@readingagency   #QuickReads

The Reading Agency Ltd. Registered number: 3904882 (England & Wales)
Registered charity number: 1085443 (England & Wales)
Registered Office: 24 Bedford Row, London, WC1R 4EH
The Reading Agency is supported using public funding by Arts Council England.

Supported using public funding by
ARTS COUNCIL
ENGLAND

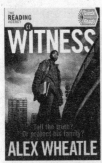

Find your next Quick Read:
the 2022 series

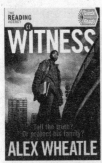

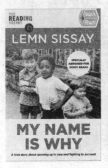

Available to buy in paperback or ebook and
to borrow from your local library.

More from Quick Reads

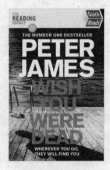

For a complete list of titles and more information
on the authors and their books visit

www.readingagency.org.uk/quickreads

Continue your reading journey

The Reading Agency is here to help keep you and your family reading:

Challenge yourself to complete six reads by taking part in **Reading Ahead** at your local library, college or workplace **readingahead.org.uk**

Join **Reading Groups for Everyone** to find a reading group and discover new books **readinggroups.org.uk**

Celebrate reading on **World Book Night** every year on 23 April **worldbooknight.org**

Read with your family as part of the **Summer Reading Challenge** at your local library **summerreadingchallenge.org.uk**

For more information, please visit our website: **readingagency.org.uk**